The
Great
Death

The
Great
Death

JOHN SMELCER

Henry Holt and Company

New York

The author would like to thank his editor, Bard Young,
as well as Rebecca Davis, Ana Deboo, David Collins,
Jaimee Colbert, and Jack Vernon.

Henry Holt and Company, LLC
Publishers since 1866
175 Fifth Avenue
New York, New York 10010
www.HenryHoltKids.com

Library of Congress Cataloging-in-Publication Data
Smelcer, John E.
The Great Death / John Smelcer.—1st ed.
p.   cm.
Summary: As their Alaskan village's only survivors of sickness
brought by white men one winter early in the twentieth century,
sisters Millie, aged thirteen, and Maura, ten, make their way
south in hopes of finding someone alive.
ISBN 978-0-8050-8100-8
[1. Sisters—Fiction.   2. Survival—Fiction.   3. Voyages and
travels—Fiction.   4. Orphans—Fiction.   5. Death—Fiction.
6. Epidemics—Fiction.   7. Indians of North America—Alaska—
Fiction.   8. Alaska—History—1867–1959—Fiction.]   I. Title.
PZ7.S6397Gre 2009   [Fic]—dc22   2008051113

First Edition—2009 / Designed by Véronique Lefèvre Sweet
Printed in September 2009 in the United States of America
by Quebecor World, Fairfield, Pennsylvania, on acid-free paper. ∞

1   3   5   7   9   10   8   6   4   2

*For John and Jane Jones, Leo Walsh,
and my grandmothers, Mary Smelcer-Wood
and Morrie Secondchief*

There is no agony like
bearing an untold story inside you.
—Zora Neale Hurston

The
Great
Death

Prologue

As Western Europeans settled Alaska, they brought with them diseases against which the indigenous peoples had no natural immunity. At the beginning of the twentieth century, fully two thirds of all Alaska Natives perished from a pandemic of measles, smallpox, and influenza. No community was spared. In most cases, half of a village's population died within a week. In some cases, there were no survivors. It was the end of an ancient way of life. Natives still refer to the dreadful period as the Great Death.

This is the story of the last two survivors of one little village, two young sisters who had to save themselves . . . and in doing so, save each other.

Ts'iłk'ey

(One)

In Yani'da'a, the long-ago time, Raven was flying around looking for something to eat. He was very hungry as usual. Once, he had even been hungry the day after he finished eating a whale.

SOME STORIES ARE TOO BIG to be told all at once, even if they seem small. Largeness of story has nothing to do with the length of each word or of each sentence or with the number of pages, but with the capacity of the heart, which can take only so much.

This is such a story.

It begins in a little-known corner of Alaska less than two decades after the end of the Klondike Gold Rush, one of America's last great adventures. Back then, there stood a small village at the northern edge of a great lake surrounded on the south side by mountains and fed by a glacier. A fast-running river flows from the far eastern side of the lake. Indeed, the name for the river in the local indigenous language, Tazlina, means "swift river."

Don't bother to look for the village on a map; you won't find it.

The People had lived in this country forever, not *forever* in the sense that a farming family that has lived on the same farm for generations would use the word, but so long as to give depth and width and the smell of age to the word.

More than two dozen families dwelled in small log houses at the edge of the lake. They weren't very tall houses, for they were built partially into the ground, which had the benefit of cooling them in summer and warming them in winter. The roofs were covered with sod, the heavy soil insulating the homes. They were abloom with weeds and wildflowers. And every green roof was adorned with weathered, gray caribou and moose antlers—some very large, for game was plentiful in those days.

Smoke from cooking fires rose and drifted through the village, helping to drive away mosquitoes, the plague of summertime, from which there was no true escape. Racks made of willow were laden with strips of red salmon hanging to dry in the sun and wind. Little houses on tall legs stood back in the forest of black spruce. These caches, accessible only by ladder, stored dried fish and meat out of the reach of animals.

Canoes were pulled up on the gravel beach. At the western edge of the village, a thin footbridge made of a fallen timber spanned a clear stream, which was full of bright red salmon. Dogs ran about barking and sniffing and searching for something to eat. Children helped their families—sons helping fathers and uncles, daughters helping mothers and aunts—or they chased the dogs along the beach or skipped rocks on the water.

In such a small village, everyone was somehow related. But on such a harsh land the amity of other villages was important. In time of famine, when the great herds of caribou did not come into the country during winter, that sense of wider community could mean the difference between life and death. Sharing in time of need is paramount in the north, where snow and quiet and darkness rule the land for half a year at a time. It is one of the most essential laws.

It was in this village that the story begins.

But it does not end there.

Several spear-holding men were standing knee-deep in the stream as it widened and shallowed, emptying into the lake. The bottom of the creek was sand and pebbles, where salmon congregated and readied themselves for their final push upstream, up to the headwater that would welcome their spawn—life arising from death as day arises from night; such is the cycle of existence.

The men stabbed salmon with the long, barbed spears, flinging them ashore to their wives, who deftly cut them open and tossed the innards back into the water so that the spirits of the salmon could return to the sea. It was important that the People respect the salmon, which they depended on to outlast the long, desolate winters. If the salmon spirits thought they had been disrespected, they might not return in the future.

Two eagles watched everything from the treetops. Seagulls hovered and mewed above the women, diving and fighting one another for whatever was flung into the moving water, and far out on the lake, ducks floated on the shimmering blue-gray surface. Even farther, on the distant horizon, the white glacier crept in the distance.

Upstream from the men was the little footbridge, and upstream of that stood two young girls, sisters— the older and taller on the right bank, the younger girl perched precariously on a large rock midstream, several other large rocks protruding from the water behind her.

"Jump!" shouted Millie from the bank. "You can make it!"

"But I can't!" Maura shouted above the din of the rushing water. "I'll fall in!"

Maura had jumped from one rock to another, but now the distance to shore seemed too great.

"You're always afraid of everything!" shouted Millie. She was impatient because her mother had asked her to fetch her younger sister. Mother would be angry at her for taking so long, even though it was Maura's fault they were late. She had stood on the boulder for a long time, too frightened to leap. But that wouldn't matter. Millie was older; it was she who would be blamed.

"I am not," replied Maura quietly, barely audible above the rushing water, almost losing her footing on the slippery rock.

But it was true. Maura wouldn't even go to the outhouse alone after dark. She always made her sister go with her, and she always sang a little song while inside, her heels nervously tapping against the boards.

Running past Millie, a lean dog chased a squirrel up a tree and then peered eagerly into the limbs, barking at the chattering escapee. It wasn't their dog. Dozens of dogs roamed the village.

"Hurry up and jump!" Millie shouted. "Mother said to come home!"

"I can't. I'll fall in," replied Maura, almost in tears, thinking of the swift, icy water.

Millie reached out her hand. "Grab hold when you jump! I'll catch you!"

Maura crouched, not nearly low enough, and jumped, landing in water up to her waist. Salmon darted from beneath and about her, splashing every which way up and down the stream, the way they do when wading bears try to pounce on them. Maura stood only a step from shore crying, the ends of her long black hair floating around her.

Millie leaned forward and helped her little sister out of the stream. "You're too frightened. You really must grow up." Her tone was stern, in a motherly sort of way, though she was only three years older. Millie even looked like their mother. Maura took after their father.

Maura stopped crying as she walked behind Millie on the narrow trail to their house, her dress dripping. Mosquitoes buzzed about them; the squirrel-chasing dog followed on their heels, stopping often to mark bushes and trees.

"But I'm only ten," she said quietly, feeling a little ashamed of herself.

"At your age, I was swimming in the lake," Millie said over her shoulder. "You're too afraid even to wade in the stream."

Maura didn't say anything for several steps but finally managed, "I can't help it if I'm small."

As she walked, Maura stretched her stride to match the prints left by her sister's moccasins on the sandy trail.

Millie stopped and turned to Maura. "The badger is small, but even the mighty bear fears him."

Neither of the girls said a word after that. The mosquitoes continued to buzz, and the dog ran off after another squirrel.

When they entered their small house, their mother was cooking fish-egg soup over an open fire, adding wild potatoes to the black cast-iron pot. The inside of the house was smoke-filled and crowded, consisting of a single room with two beds mounted along the hewn-log walls. A small table stood under the only window in the cabin. Now, at midday, the table was bare, except for an unlit candle and a box of matches. Two rickety chairs flanked the table's end, though it served a family of four.

No art adorned the walls, no pictures of any kind, no photographs. There were no books, no fine china, no dolls or other playthings of any sort, no cupboards or toilets or closets. The floor was earthen but clean-swept. A lever-action rifle leaned in a corner below a dozen traps hanging from nails, a box of cartridges on the floor beneath it. On one wall hung three beaver pelts and a great many smaller muskrat and marten furs; on the opposite wall hung two wolf hides. The home smelled of tanned leather and wood smoke. A large bear hide was stretched and nailed on a wall outside, dry and cracked from the sun and wind.

"*There* you are," their mother said without turning.

Millie steeled herself for Mother's reaction.

"I told you to go find your sister a long time ago. What took you so long? I had to gather the firewood and prepare the soup by myself."

Then Mother looked over her shoulder and saw that Maura was soaking wet.

"What happened to her?" she shouted at Millie.

Millie tried to explain that she couldn't find Maura at first, that she had finally seen her playing on the other side of the creek, and that when they crossed the creek above the bridge, her little sister had fallen into the water.

"It's your responsibility to watch after your sister," Mother said sternly, stirring the pot with a rough, hand-carved wooden spoon. "How many times have I told you that you must take care of her?"

Millie looked at the earthen floor. She couldn't look at her mother's face, couldn't bear to see the disappointment wrinkling her forehead.

Millie hated looking after Maura. She wanted to sew

and bead and sit with other older girls as they tanned moose and caribou hides for leather to make moccasins, gossiping all the while about boys. It wasn't fair that she had to spend so much of her time keeping an eye on Maura.

Sometimes, Millie hated her little sister.

Nadaeggi
(Two)

Raven was flying around when he saw a village at the edge of the frozen sea. He landed and spoke to the chief of the village.

"Oh, wise chief," he said cunningly, "the village up the coast is planning to attack your village."

The old chief was very concerned. "What shall we do?" he asked.

A COMMOTION AROSE at the lakefront. Dogs were barking, and everyone in the village was running to see what the excitement was. Millie and Maura raced down the little hill and joined the crowd, most of whom were standing along the upper beach watching three men approach the village. Still far away, they walked along the shore from the direction where the river begins, about a mile down the lake.

"Who is it?" an old woman asked.

A boy replied, "I don't know, grandmother. I can't see them from here."

"Is it a chief from downriver?" someone else asked.

Every village had a chief.

The elder men talked among themselves and quickly agreed to dispatch several young men to meet the approaching party halfway. They ran along the path that meandered close to the lakeshore. On reaching the men, they stopped and spoke briefly to them, and then the group walked together to the village, several of the loose dogs sniffing the strangers.

One of the men was from a village downriver. He was a cousin to several older villagers, and they clasped his hands when they saw him. But the two men with him were strange-looking. Their skin was light, almost white. One had red hair, while the other's hair was like that of a light-colored grizzly bear. Both had blue eyes!

Millie and Maura had never seen anyone like them before, though they had heard of such people in stories told by the men who sometimes left the village to go downriver to trade their furs for large sacks of flour and dried beans and tea and other goods, such as small glass windows, iron cooking kettles, metal axes, saws, guns, bullets, knives, and steel animal traps.

The two girls pressed through the crowd so that they could see better and hear the conversation. They wondered if the men were friendly or if they meant harm. The strangers were taller than any man in the village by a head. Their clothes were different. Their boots were different. Even the outsiders' words were different. No one in the village understood what they were saying. The strangers had to speak first to the man from downriver, who turned and spoke to the villagers in their language, even though some of his words sounded a little different because he spoke another dialect.

The white men asked how many people lived in the village, how many men and women and children. They asked if there were other villages farther up the wide valley. The chief, an old man whose hair was mostly gray, answered the man from downriver, who turned to tell the strangers, one of whom quickly scrawled a little stick against broad, white leaves bound in hide, which he had retrieved from a rucksack.

"Have you any news?" the chief asked the man from downriver.

The man coughed into his hand a few times before answering.

"Yes," he said, clearing his throat. "Many of the old ones have died this summer. So have some of the very young. It has been a bad time."

Then he began to recite the names of the dead. Some were relatives of those who stood quietly listening, shocked by the long list. They had seen some of those very people only the previous spring.

"What can we do to help?" the chief asked.

"Nothing," replied the other Indian. He looked to be a few years older than Millie and Maura's father, who was standing beside the old chief. "Our shaman exhausted himself trying to heal the people. But then, old as he was, he too died from the sickness, and now we have no shaman. Death is everywhere, in every house."

The shaman from Millie and Maura's village had died of old age during the winter. Some people said he was ninety years old.

The man coughed again, harder this time, and wiped his forehead with the back of his hand. Little red spots dotted his hands and arms, which no one had noticed until then. Neither Maura nor Millie had seen such spots on a person before. Millie wondered if he had been bitten by a hundred mosquitoes.

One of the strangers, the red-haired man, reached into his pack and pulled out a brown wooden box. The other man untied something from the side of his pack. It had three wooden legs, which he stretched out longer and longer. The red-haired man set the box atop the three-legged device. He looked closely at the thing, his fingers working little levers and dials. Then he spoke to the man from downriver, who told everyone to stand close together while the man squatted behind the device.

Millie and Maura giggled. Others laughed as well. The strange red-haired man looked funny hunched behind the box, glancing up and motioning for the people to move closer together.

A sharp sound came from the box, like the snap of a dry twig when it's broken and thrown into the cooking fire. *Click*. Maura grabbed Millie's hand, frightened by the noise, but when nothing happened, she let go. After a moment, the man looked up, lifted the thing—legs, box, and all—and moved it a few steps closer and to the side before hunkering behind it again. *Click*.

Both men then walked around the village, setting up the device here and there, the man with light brown hair continually scrawling on the white hide. Most of the villagers followed them, curious about what they were doing and what it was the man saw of such great interest inside the little box. Perhaps it was some sort of ritual. Sometimes the men asked villagers to stand before a cabin or a tall cache or a rack full of drying salmon. Sometimes they asked individuals to squat beside a dog or a canoe. They asked Millie and Maura's father to stand beside the bearskin stretched and nailed to the outside wall of their cabin. It was a very large skin, at least nine feet long. Then the red-haired man gestured for Millie and Maura to stand alongside a dogsled with tall grass and fireweed growing up through its runners. When they didn't understand, he took them by the shoulders and gently pushed them closer to the sled. Maura didn't like the man touching her, but she moved all the same.

After a while, the women began to prepare a great meal. The men and children followed the strangers, watching them curiously. It seemed like every dog in the village sniffed them. A few kept their distance, barking until someone led them away and tied them up. Smoke from a dozen fires drifted in the air. Everyone was busy. Millie and Maura helped their mother, while some of the other children continued to follow the strangers around the village. Both girls wanted to be outside too, but Mother insisted that they help her with the preparations. The man from downriver spent most of his time speaking with the men of the village and visiting in the homes of some of his relatives, talking about those who had died.

When the sun hung low on the edge of the horizon, the women and girls began to carry food into the community house, a long log house in the middle of the village used for special events and ceremonies, like the potlatch—a ritual involving feasting, dancing, singing, and the giving away of gifts to strengthen the bonds between kinsmen and clans and villages. They brought boiled porcupine and beaver, roasted bear and moose meat, roasted and dried salmon, and pots of fish-head soup. Maura carried a birch-bark basket partially filled with blueberries and cranberries, for they were ripe in the hills, while Millie carried a basket brimming with golden-brown fry bread, her favorite.

Everyone was smiling and talking about the visitors and how good the food smelled. When everything was ready, the entire village joined in the feast welcoming the guests. There hadn't been such a celebration since before the snow melted in the spring. After supper, elder men sang and drummed while the People danced—the men and boys in the center of the circle, women and girls in the outer circle, as was the custom. Millie and Maura took turns dancing and carrying their baby cousin, speaking to him softly, rocking him in their arms, and smiling. People thanked the man from downriver for bringing the news, for though it was unhappy news—and so heavily received—they would not have known otherwise. In this rugged country, word traveled slowly, like the distant glacier, or not at all.

That night the three visitors slept in the community house, and the next morning, the strangers and their guide, who looked very sick indeed, began the long trek downriver. Millie and Maura stood among the people on the beachfront watching as the party disappeared down the trail along the lapping lake's edge. The sisters wondered if they'd ever see the mysterious men again. They wondered about the hundred mosquito bites on the man from downriver.

"Do you think they itch?" Maura whispered to Millie, imagining how terrible it would be if they all itched at the same time.

The villagers were thankful to have had guests, to have welcomed them properly and according to tradition, even thankful in their own way to have received the grim news. Several of the village dogs followed the men for a ways but eventually turned around and trotted home.

When the strangers were no longer visible, the villagers returned to the busy work of survival, catching and drying salmon, repairing snowshoes and dogsleds, collecting and sawing firewood, scraping and tanning hides, and mending and fashioning warm clothes against the winter, which still seemed far away, biding its time in the distant white mountains, nestled against glaciers, awaiting its coming release to the world.

The People always prepared against death, for they knew how it crept steadily down the mountains toward them.

"Life goes on," they thought as they busied themselves with work. "Life always goes on."

Taa'i

(Three)

Raven had a wicked plan. "You must ambush the enemy on their way to your village," he said, his black eyes blinking. "You must catch them by surprise."

"Where shall we wait to ambush them?" asked the chief, thankful for Raven's help.

THE GREAT DEATH BEGAN on a cloudless fall day. Geese flying overhead on their long journey south called down to the People, telling them farewell. Others, resting on a far shoreline, turned into the wind, clambered into the sky, and joined their cousins.

Several days after the strange men left the village, the chief awoke with small red spots all over his body. Since there was no shaman in the village, some of the old women rubbed bear grease and ash on his skin and gave him weak tea made from the leaf of a local plant to drink. The men readied a steam bath hot enough to drive out the sickness. One of his sons even made him a pot of bear-heart soup, a traditional remedy to bolster courage and vigor.

Two days later, some of the other men had the spots, then their children and their wives. In a week, almost everyone in the village had red spots like the man from downriver who had guided the strangers. Everyone remembered what the man had said about the deaths in his village.

"The very old and the very young," he had said.

But they also remembered how sickly the man had looked when he left with the two white men. Death trudged along the path beside that man like a shadow, like a huge tiredness hanging off his shoulders. The people began to worry that whatever had befallen the village downriver was now upon them.

At first the spots were unpleasant to look at but they were not debilitating. But day after day, the infected grew increasingly weary, until the entire village could be divided in half: those who were too weak to work or move about and those who looked after them. No one was hunting or cutting firewood or picking berries. No one was catching fish for the winter, though the salmon splashed weakly in the shallow stream, spawned out and dying. Their bodies were growing blood-red, their heads dark green, their mouths gnarled and hooked.

Because there was so little activity throughout the village, bears grew bold, wading in the shallow creek below the footbridge to catch salmon. Soon, the creek banks were lined with partially eaten salmon, rotting and maggot-infested. Flies were everywhere, and the smell brought more bears.

Some of the more fearless bears stole salmon from the drying racks, the people's vital winter supply. The village dogs tried to drive them away, but the bears were unafraid. Bears, and especially wolves, were known to eat dogs, and so the dogs relented.

Then the chief died. Everyone mourned his passing, but they were too sick to honor him with a potlatch, too sick even to bury him. His wife died two days later. Then four other elders died, and then the babies began to die, and then the children. Winter had descended only partially down the hills, and yet death was among them.

It was a season out of season.

For reasons no one understood, least of all the girls or their parents, Millie and Maura were unaffected by the plague. Perhaps, said one old woman between hacking coughs, the owl, that harbinger of death, simply could not see them. But no one could say for sure.

The girls stayed in their house caring for their parents. Father had been among the first of the strong men to be stricken. The red spots were all over him. His body was always hot or cold, afire or shivering. Mother wasn't as sick, though she also had the spots, but she was too weak to haul water or cook meals. Maura wiped sweat from Father's face when he was hot, covered him with blankets when he was cold. Millie swept the earthen floor and cooked meals, though neither parent would eat or drink anything. She had to force herself to eat.

"We have to stay strong for Mother and Father," she told Maura, who had also lost her appetite. "We have to take care of them."

The fresh water and firewood ran out. Millie turned to Maura and said with hesitation in her voice, "We need to fetch water and firewood, and the honey bucket is full."

In their sickness, both parents were using a bucket, too weak to walk to the outhouse.

Maura went to the door, opened it, and looked out over the village to the milky blue-gray lake beyond.

"I wish Father would get better," she said sadly. "If he did, we could all go away somewhere. Mother can still walk a little. We could all go away."

She twirled some hair that hung limp over her shoulder. She often did that when she was nervous or afraid.

"Wishing will not make Father better," Millie replied. "We have to keep him clean and warm and offer food. We have to get water and firewood and empty the honey bucket. Mother is too weak to do it."

Millie turned back toward her father and felt the burn of tears welling up, not for her father or mother, not for herself, but for her little sister, who stood like a shadow in the doorway. Suddenly she no longer hated the idea of watching after Maura, who was too small, too young, too frightened, and who now must help care for their parents. She wanted to help Maura.

Maura turned from the door and stood over the bucket, holding her breath as she looked at the contents. Emptying the honey bucket was the worst chore. The sloshing liquid always threatened to spill out.

When Millie came over to her, Maura gripped her sister's forearm.

"Are they going to die?" Maura whispered, looking at their sick parents, her voice rising slightly.

"Stop it, Maura," Millie said gently but firmly, pulling her arm free. "We need to fetch water and firewood. We must do what must be done."

Millie gingerly lifted the honey bucket, and Maura grabbed the empty water pail. They would go together. The girls always left the house together now. They had heard the sounds of bears splashing in the river, prowling near the village, and the sounds of weeping and lament from nearby homes. They were afraid to go outside, especially very early or very late. Everyone in the village was afraid. They feared each day as much as each night.

Horror is most visible in daylight.

As they moved quietly toward the door, so as not to disturb their parents, Father sat up, coughing, and pointed toward the corner. "Wait. Take my rifle," he said hoarsely.

Millie carefully set down the honey bucket, picked up the rifle by the barrel with both hands, and carried it to her father.

"But I don't know how to shoot it," she said.

"Bullets," he croaked, motioning to where the box lay on the ground beside a double-headed ax.

Maura brought him the box.

Although he was very weak and his spotted hands shook terribly, Father took a bullet from the box and slid it into the loading gate.

"You try," he said, addressing Millie.

Maura watched intently, setting down the empty water pail. Mother leaned up on her elbow and watched too.

Millie tried to force the cartridge in backward.

"The other way." Father coughed, his body trembling.

Millie turned the brass cartridge around and pushed it into the loading gate until it clicked shut.

"It holds five," Father said softly, closing his eyes while Millie loaded more bullets into the rifle. Then he opened his eyes again, startled, as if he had forgotten something.

"Load a round into the chamber," he said. "Grab that lever and pull down on it."

Millie held the rifle against her thigh and pressed down on the lever, which broke open easily. The whole top of the gun seemed to slide apart.

"Now pull it back up," said Father. "Good. Careful. It's loaded now."

Father taught Millie and Maura how to safely lower the hammer when they weren't ready to shoot. He showed them how to aim, warning them to hold the butt firmly against their small, bony shoulders, and how to look down the barrel to align the sights. He taught them never to aim the barrel at anything they didn't want to kill. He was too weak to take them outside to practice. Besides, he had only half a box of ammunition. He had meant to trade some furs for more.

After the short lesson, Father fell asleep, his breathing hard.

Millie slung the rifle over her shoulder and lifted the sloshing honey bucket. She felt safer with the gun firmly pressing against her back. Maura grabbed the water pail, and together they stepped outside. No one was moving about. It was as if the entire village were asleep or, perhaps, abandoned. First they emptied the honey bucket in the outhouse, returning afterward to set the empty bucket outside the door. Then the girls walked toward the lake to fill the water pail. Now they could hear wailing and crying as they passed cabins. Death was everywhere.

When they stopped by one house to check on a friend of Millie's, they learned that another infant and two elders had died in the village during the night, too young or too old or too weak to fight off sickness for long. Millie's friend had the red spots, and she was weak and coughing. She was looking after her mother, who was lying on the bed, covered with spots and shaking terribly.

"She'll be all right," she said, wiping her mother's forehead with a wet rag. "I think she's a little better than she was this morning."

Millie and Maura thought the woman looked worse than their mother.

"Where is your father?" Millie asked.

"He died yesterday," she said. "My uncles took his body away."

Millie worried about her own father, and she wanted to hurry back to him.

"We have to go now," she said, nervously. "We must take care of our parents."

Though neither said a word as they left the cabin, Millie and Maura felt guilty that they didn't have any sign of the sickness. As far as they knew, they were the only ones in the entire village.

The People had always buried their dead, but since

the sickness arrived, no one was strong enough to drag away the corpses or to dig the many graves. Instead, they tried to burn the corpses, thinking it would kill the disease, but no one was strong enough to gather the great quantities of wood needed for funeral pyres. As the girls slowly passed nearby houses, they saw partially burned corpses lying scattered atop too-small fires, some still smoldering. They even saw the scorched body of Millie's friend's father. Millie and Maura turned their heads, frightened by the burned and disfigured faces of people they had known all their lives, many of them relatives.

They were too shocked to speak. Maura vomited twice. Millie held it back, barely, though more than once she felt it rush up into her mouth.

The dead lay everywhere—inside, outside—the dying sitting or lying beside them, the living brushing away flies from the bodies and holding cloths to their faces to lessen the stench of decay that rose from their dead and from the rotting salmon along the creek. The village that was all the girls knew of life and place and home had transformed into a smoky shadow of death.

Millie and Maura walked close together, careful to step around the dead. Millie halted when she saw the body of an older boy whom she had liked. Then she pushed on. The girls made their way down to the lake, wary of bears, filled the pail with water, and collected dry driftwood from along the beach.

No wind blew over the land. The surface of the lake was flat. A raft of mud ducks bobbed on the milky-blue water.

Millie motioned for her sister to pause with her before turning back. She looked around, at the hills, the distant mountains to the south, the broad, flat, silent lake. To Millie it seemed almost beautiful, in spite of the horror. On such a day, village children might have played in the lake or along its banks, staying close to shore, frightening one another with stories of monsters that were said to live in the lake. Father had seen one when he was a young man. He had told the story of how he was paddling his canoe along the western shoreline, looking for caribou or moose or beaver, when a giant, scaly fish, longer than his canoe, swam alongside, splashed, and dived. It was unlike anything he had ever seen. Others had seen it, too.

Was the great fish also dead, killed by the red spots?

Was all the world dying?

Denc'i

(Four)

"There is a steep cliff two days up the coast,"
said that sly Raven. "You must make camp at
the bottom of the cliff and await my signal."
Raven smiled as he lied to the chief, happy that
his deception was working. He was an accom-
plished liar.

A DOG TROTTED BY on the beach carrying something
in its mouth. It lay down and began eating, tearing off
pieces with its teeth. The girls thought it was a salmon at
first, but when they were close enough, they realized that
they were wrong. They could see fingers.

Millie picked up a stone from the beach and hurled it
at the dog, striking it squarely in the side. But it didn't
move. It kept eating, greedily gulping pieces. Both girls

dropped their bundles of firewood and ran at the dog, yelling and waving their arms.

"Go away!" they shouted. "Go away!"

The dog stood up, growling at the meddlesome girls. Millie picked up another stone and hurled it with all her strength, hitting the dog again. This time it dropped the arm and skulked back toward the village with its tail between its legs.

The dogs were eating the dead. For many days, no one had been feeding the dogs, and so, hungry as they were, they turned to the only food they could find.

Millie and Maura picked up their bundles of wood and the pail of fresh water and returned to their house. Father was still asleep. Mother was awake but too weak to sit up.

"Daughters," Mother said hoarsely, as if her words were dying, as if they too had red spots, "go check on my sister and her baby."

Auntie had given birth in early spring, when the ice melted on the lake. Both mother and child had caught the sickness the day after Millie and Maura's father first showed the spots. Uncle had been among the first men to die.

Before leaving as Mother asked, the sisters rekindled the fire, warming the cabin. Maura washed her mother's face, tried to get her to drink some water. She studied the tattoo on Mother's chin: three blue-black lines running vertically from just below her lower lip. All the women in the village had tattoos on their faces, some of the lines solid, some dotted, but all the same color. It was a sign of beauty and maturity, of reaching the marrying age. The lines were made by stitching strings of gut smeared with bear grease and ash into the skin, leaving the permanent blue-black lines after the stitches fell out.

"Are you cold?" Maura asked Mother gently.

"No, child." Her mother did not open her eyes to speak, but she trembled from time to time, as if shivering. Maura pulled the blanket a little higher and looked closely at her mother's face, tracing the tattoo softly with a finger.

One day, she thought, *Millie and I will have tattoos.* Then she began to cry a little, quietly, not letting her sister see her. It was a mother's role along with her sisters and other women of the village to sew the stitches. Maura worried that her mother wouldn't be here to do this for her. She was afraid that no one would be here.

Father was asleep. As Millie checked on him, his lungs rattled in his chest like a crumpled, dry fish skin. When she was certain he was still alive, she took up the rifle and motioned to Maura that it was time to leave.

Mother spoke to Millie. "Watch after your sister."

She said that whenever they left the house.

"I will, Mother," Millie replied sadly. She wondered if this might be the last time she answered her mother's constant demand. Though she could not cure her mother, Millie could promise this one thing to her.

Auntie lived on the far side of the village. On the way the two sisters saw more partially burned bodies of friends and relatives, blackened and rank, dogs feasting on the charred remains, ravens and magpies picking at them. Each time the girls approached, the birds fluttered away momentarily and then resettled on their meals. Millie thought about using her gun to stop the animals. But was Millie to shoot them all? Every dog? Every bird?

There were bear tracks all around the village. No sounds came from inside the cabins they passed. Either no one was alive or no one was speaking—no one comforting the dying. Comfort didn't help anyway.

The living still died. The dead stayed dead.

And the stench!

The smell of rotting flesh, both salmon and human, crouched on the village like a thick, living fog, so full of decay it was as if the air itself were squirming with maggots. Occasionally, a breeze would arise and sweep the pungency from the village and out across the lake.

Although little else stirred, the maddening clouds of mosquitoes still whined and bit.

When they approached Auntie's cabin, the girls were relieved to hear the muted sound of a baby crying weakly. At least two other people in the village were yet alive, they thought. But when they opened the door, their relief fled like squirrels from an angry dog. Auntie lay sprawled on the earthen floor, her blouse open, her naked baby lying atop her, suckling listlessly on a spotted, lifeless breast, crying because he was hungry, his little shuddering body covered with the red death.

Maura picked up her cousin, laid him on the bed, wrapped him in a blanket, and sang to him softly, trying to calm him, while Millie tried to feed him water squeezed from a dampened rag. His entire body was covered with red spots, even his eyelids. This was the same baby they had played with joyously during the pot-latch celebration the night the strangers arrived. After a few minutes, the baby stopped crying. Darkness was gathering outside. It was getting quite dim in the cabin. Millie lit a candle and brought it close to the bed.

The two girls sat on the rickety bed while Maura held the baby, watching helplessly as his breathing slowed and then stopped altogether, his fixed brown eyes staring at the dark.

Maura suddenly grasped her sister's arm.

"He isn't dead, is he? He'll be all right, won't he? We can take him with us. He'll—"

"Stop it, Maura!" Millie's voice was loud and stunned them both. "He is dead." Her words trembled as she continued. "We can't do anything for him. We should go home now and tell Mother."

The sisters carefully lifted their dead aunt and laid her body on the bed, setting her baby, still wrapped in a blanket, in her arms.

Millie stood, grabbed the rifle, and blew out the candle. She guided her little sister outside by the shoulder, closed the cabin door tightly so that dogs couldn't get in, and then she and Maura began to walk home without saying a word, too overcome by the burden of death and sadness. The stench in the village was insufferable. They felt as though they could not breathe. They were afraid to breathe.

Even the air was sick.

Arriving back home, Millie turned to her sister before she opened the door.

"You have to be strong now," she said, but not in the harsh, chastising tone she had used before. There was a soft urgency in her voice, a pointing out of the necessary.

Maura looked away, tears welling in her eyes. "I know" was all she could muster.

Mother was awake. She had been waiting for their return. Father was sleeping. Millie added some wood to the fire while Maura lit a candle.

"Mother," Millie whispered, leaning over her mother's face, "Auntie is dead. So is her baby."

Tears streamed down her mother's cheeks. The girls cried, too, as their mother's grief opened the door to their own.

That night, a bear tried to get inside the cabin. At first they could hear it snuffling and grunting. Then it scratched at the walls and at the door.

"It's trying to get in," Maura whispered, clutching her mother's hand, her voice trembling.

Millie sat up half the night drowsily aiming the rifle at the door. Maura kept the fire burning and the ax close. Eventually the bear wandered off. The girls' parents slept fitfully, waking up frequently in coughing spasms. Maura finally dozed off, and even Millie's head slumped forward, her chin resting on the shoulder that hugged the heavy rifle's butt.

Outside, stars clustered like mosquitoes and the moonless night dwindled into nothingness—and within the nothingness, rising to the stars, were a multitude of spirits of the dead.

ʼAltsʼeni

(Five)

*After the chief explained Raven's plan to his
people, he told them to prepare for the journey.
As the villagers packed their supplies and readied their dogsleds, Raven flew away, cawing
and cawing loudly, which was his way of
laughing.*

THE GIRLS' MOTHER DIED in spasms, her convulsions
on the thin bed waking Millie and Maura near morning.
They tended to her as best they could, trying to hold her
still, wiping her with cool water, crying and telling her
how much they loved her.

But love wasn't strong enough to stop the Great
Death.

Only after Mother's violent death did the girls notice

that Father had already died. His body was cold and stiff. He had passed quietly sometime during the endless night. The sisters were orphans now, without other adults to turn to. They were exhausted, not simply from lack of sleep but from the unrelenting burden of sorrow heaped on sorrow.

Maura began to cry, only a little at first, then uncontrollably—her small body shuddering in great sobbing heaves. Although it was her people's custom to hold back sentiment, to be as strong as the pitiless land itself, she couldn't do so any longer. She ran to Millie, threw her arms around her waist, and wept with her face pressed against her sister's heart.

It was too much even for Millie, who felt the first tears roll down her cheek, tasted tearsalt. There was a growing tightness in her chest, as if a strong hand gripped her heart so fiercely that her lungs were afraid to breathe. A great wave of helplessness drowned her. She held her sister close, and they cried for a long time.

"What do we do with Mother and Father?" asked Maura finally, wiping tears from her cheeks with the palms of her hands and kneeling by the fire.

"We need to bury them so the dogs and birds and

bears won't eat them," answered Millie. "We can't bury everyone else, but we must bury our parents."

Maura stood up, brushing dirt from the back of her long dress. She opened her mouth to speak but could not. She wanted to ask her sister how they could live and continue. She grabbed the shovel and the ax from beside the door. Only then did she find her voice.

"We'll need these," she said, her eyes bloodshot from crying and from weariness.

The ax would cut stubborn, shallow spruce tree roots, which did not reach deep but spread out, clutching their fingers into the soil against high winds that sometimes blew across the lake, uprooting trees. The village was built on an ancient lakeshore made of mostly sand and gravel. Although it was late fall and the ground was cold, it would not be difficult to dig in.

Millie took up the rifle, slung it over a shoulder, opened the door, and looked around warily.

They decided to bury their parents behind the house. They took turns hacking out roots and digging. They dug only one hole, but cut it deep enough so that the dogs wouldn't undo their work.

When the grave was ready, the girls returned to the

house and rolled Mother and Father, one at a time, onto a blanket and dragged them out the door and around to the back of the cabin. They lowered each parent into the hole and filled the grave. They breathed hard from their labor but said nothing. Both were lost in their own thoughts. They listened to the sound of the shovels scooping dirt, a squirrel chattering in a distant tree. When finished, they stamped on the surface, packing the earth below.

It was a good burial. Their parents would have been proud.

Afterward, the girls sat inside their cabin, resting from the miserable task. Millie thought of Father sitting by the fire in the evenings tanning beaver and marten hides, telling stories while he worked. Maura thought of Mother preparing meals with the girls, and sitting on the edge of the bed each night combing out Maura's long hair.

"What should we do now?" Maura asked, drinking a ladleful of lake water from the pail, then wiping her mouth on her long sleeve.

Millie also took a drink before replying.

"We have to leave this place. If we linger, we may yet

catch the sickness ourselves. But first we should search the village for survivors. It won't be easy, but we have to, I think."

Maura agreed, though neither had seen or heard anyone moving about all morning as they'd dug their parents' grave.

"It would be terrible to leave someone behind," Millie continued. "I know it will be hard for you, Maura. I dread this too. But you just helped me bury Mother and Father. You're stronger than you think you are."

Maura smiled a little, the first time she had smiled in a long while, and straightened her back.

After drinking some weak tea, the girls began the search. Millie carried the rifle, and Maura carried the ax. At first whenever they opened a cabin door, the overwhelming stench caused both girls to convulse. Maura threw up again, and Millie's stomach swooped like a small bird on the wind. But after a few times, they learned to cover their mouths and turn away. The sight of the dead was ghastly, each corpse contorted and bloated, covered with red spots and flies and maggots. They tried to avoid seeing the grimaces. It was better that way. These were the faces of friends, close and distant relatives, people who had been kind to them, and people whom they had not liked very much.

But the most terrible thing they saw fueled their worst imaginings. Bear tracks of different shapes and sizes surrounded the cabin at the farthest edge of the village. Millie thought she could count the tracks of three or four bears. She said nothing, but kept the rifle ready.

The family who lived in the cabin included a grandmother and two children. Maura had sometimes played with the children, who were close to her age, and the old woman had taught Millie how to make bead necklaces. The door was wide open. Clothing and blankets and pots and pans were strewn all over the yard.

The girls braced themselves before looking inside. They knew it would be bad, but it was worse than they'd imagined. There was no sign of the family, no stiff and spotted bodies, but the earthen floor was soaked a dark reddish-brown, almost black. And flies swarmed on everything.

Millie surmised that bears had dragged the bodies into the nearby woods. Grizzly bears often move large game, like a moose or a deer, to a safe place where they can eat what they want in peace, burying the rest for later. There are even stories of people who had been mauled by a bear and left for dead, only to awaken partially buried in the cooling soil.

Millie closed the door, and then she and Maura finished checking the rest of the houses, calling out the names of the people who lived in each one as they peered through a window or opened a door. No one answered. No one else was alive in the entire village. Even Millie's friend who had been looking after her mother was dead.

"What should we do now?" asked Maura for the second time. "Where shall we go?"

Millie had been thinking about the question even while they buried Mother and Father.

"We have to go downriver," she said. "It's our only choice. We'll take one of the canoes."

For the rest of the day, Millie and Maura took what they needed from the homes of their dead relatives, neighbors, and friends. There were some cabins they refused to return to, such was the horror and stench. For the most part they searched houses near their own, averting their gaze from the dead, taking what they needed quickly, holding their breath as long as they could, ever vigilant for bears.

Millie had to reassure Maura frequently.

"I know it's hard," she said before they went into their aunt's cabin, "but we have to get supplies. We won't survive without them."

They found more bullets for their father's rifle. Maura took a small-caliber rifle for herself, a rabbit-and-grouse gun. They gathered bedding, pots and pans, axes, traps and snares, rope, and a long shovel. They collected hunting knives, candles, matches, and bundles of dried salmon from a cache that had escaped pillage by the animals and by the sick and starving. They found boxes of salt, good for preserving fish or meat. They even found a white canvas tarp, which folded out to a dozen feet square—perfect for pitching over a pole for shelter against rain, snow, and wind. One of the men in the village had traded furs for it. The girls folded it up, guided by the deep creases, and tied it crisscross with a short rope.

In their hurry to gather supplies, Millie worried that she might forget something important.

From their own house the girls took winter clothes Mother and Auntie had made for them: two warm parkas, the hoods trimmed with wolf fur; mittens and mukluks trimmed with the fur of black bears, caribou, wolves, and beavers. Beaver fur was best for winter.

Millie knew that winter was impatient to throw itself onto the world.

They carefully packed everything into two wooden boxes. One was a waist-high steamer trunk with a lockable clasp. The other was long and flat and rectangular. Although the girls could not read them, words on the side of the crate said that the box had contained a dozen long-handled shovels shipped from Seattle and then transported over plains and mountains to gold camps. Whereas the gold pan and the sluice box were vital to toiling, weary gold-seekers, the shovel was the most indispensable tool of all.

The girls managed to drag the boxes, one at a time, to the edge of the lake. A grizzly approached while they were packing the canoe, walking noiselessly along the beach, shaking its massive, shaggy head. Millie fired a shot at the bear and missed—the bullet whizzed harmlessly over its head. But it was enough to frighten the bear away.

So late in the fall, the sun fell quickly behind the mountains. By sundown, they had filled the belly of the long canoe with enough provisions to help them endure the coming hardships of the wilderness. It was too late and too dark to navigate the river. They would set off in the morning.

The girls took the bundles of dried salmon into the house so that they wouldn't attract hungry dogs or bears.

That night, Millie and Maura slept lightly, tossing from nightmares, waking often, despite their fatigue, eventually drifting back into a restless sleep only to dream once again of the horrors of the long day. As they turned in their blankets inside their cabin, warmed by a small, crackling fire, low clouds blew down from the north, and the moon gleamed white and cold through breaks in the cloud cover. Sometime around midnight, the first sign of winter arrived in the valley, hushed as a lemming.

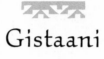

Gistaani

(Six)

Two days later, the villagers arrived at the place Raven had described. They made camp at the base of the steep cliff and waited for Raven's signal. But that sly Raven flew to the top of the cliff, where a great overhang of snow loomed above the camp.

WHEN THE FIRST FLURRY of snow fell briefly—when it lay swirled lightly on the gravel beach and on the sod roofs of houses, when it made the footbridge treacherous, when the white covering crunched underfoot thin enough that it would surely melt under the same day's sun, when the creeks and rivers and ponds were still without ice, when restless bears first gave thought to their musty winter dens—then the sisters abandoned their village, now more cemetery than home.

Millie was the first to awaken in the morning. She looked out the small window and saw the world whitened during the night.

"Wake up," she said to her sister, shaking her. "Wake up."

Maura opened her eyes and looked up at Millie, trying to focus the world.

"It snowed last night. We have to leave."

Millie was afraid the lake and the river might freeze. But of course it was much too early for that. She pulled the heavy blankets from her sister, who quickly curled into a ball. It was cold inside the cabin. Neither had got up in the night to keep the fire burning.

"Get up, Maura. We must go."

Maura whimpered. "Can't we sleep just a little longer?" Her own voice ruined her foggy detachment. Even before Millie replied, she forced herself to sit up, wiping the crusty flakes of sleep from her eyelids.

"No. Come on and help me." Millie tried to sound firm and sure of herself without scolding.

From the corner of her eye she watched her little sister begin to move about. How small and frail she seemed, draped in her nightshirt. Mother and Father were gone.

Millie hadn't been able to save them. But there was one thing she could still do for them—for Mother, especially. She could take care of Maura. Watching her sister fumble with her clothes, Millie made a vow. She would be strong for both of them. She would keep Maura safe. Thinking of the long trip ahead, Millie had to stiffen herself to keep from trembling. She had to tell herself over and over to be strong, like the wolverine or even the weasel, which is fierce for its size.

The girls dressed warmly. Then they boiled a pot of weak tea and ate some of the dried salmon from the bundles they had found in the undisturbed cache. They stood in the doorway of their small house, looking inside one last time, both thinking of happier days. It had been their home for all of their lives. Then they went around to the back of the cabin to say good-bye to Mother and Father. Shortly thereafter, they were standing on the beach, their blankets and dried salmon loaded into the canoe. The white tarp was unfolded just enough to cover their provisions from the wet snow.

After steadying the canoe so that Maura could make her way to the bow, Millie shoved it away from the beach and jumped in, the boat momentarily rocking side to side. The girls paddled toward the river outlet a mile away, looking back at the gravel shoreline and their village, at the vast surrounding wilderness—the frontier of the world. They suddenly felt small and lonely.

The girls knew from their father and others that there was a village many days downriver. It was from that village that the Indian guide had brought the two strange men . . . and the sickness. Millie and Maura wondered if everyone there was already dead. Beyond that, there was said to be a large settlement where many of the men in the village went to trade. Father said the settlement was full of white people like the ones who had come to visit. It was very far away, at the confluence where the river emptied into a much larger river. Millie and Maura had no idea how long their journey would be, or if there would even be anyone left to greet them.

Snowflakes swirled in the light wind and melted when they landed on the canoe. The temperature had risen somewhat, and this first snow could not hold its grip.

At the river outlet, they came within view of a small cabin that belonged to an old man whose wife had died several years before. In his grief, he had built this house away from the rest of the community. Sorrow craves solitude. The old man was a first cousin to the man from downriver who had guided the strange white men. No doubt they had stopped at his cabin before walking the last mile into the village. Perhaps he had made a pot of tea for them and offered them something to eat.

From their canoe, the girls could see two dogs tied up to a tree in the front yard of the house. The door was wide open.

Millie dug the oar in deep, back-paddling enough to turn the bow toward the cabin. Perhaps the old man had escaped the sickness. Perhaps he was still alive. Yet they had not seen him in the village since the day the visitors left. Also, he would have been the first and last person on the lake to have seen the strangers as they passed by his cabin at the head of the trail downriver. . . .

When the canoe landed softly, Millie jumped out and pulled the bow onto the beach. The dogs sat up and barked. Millie grabbed her rifle from atop the pile of supplies.

"Stay here," she warned Maura, gesturing with a hand for her to remain seated in the canoe.

Millie approached the cabin cautiously, calling out the

old man's name as she walked up the worn trail. The dogs stopped barking. Instead, they whined and wagged their tails. When she was close, Millie could see that they were thin and starving. Their ribs showed through their mangy fall coats. She called out for the old man again. The only reply was the dogs' whimperings and Maura's voice from the canoe.

"Is he there?" Maura asked. "Is anyone home?"

Millie stepped close to the door and looked in warily, her rifle ready. The cabin was empty. Nothing was disturbed. There was no sign of anyone, no sign of a struggle. Had he escaped the sickness? But why had he left the door open, the dogs tied fast to a tree without food or water? Surely they would have accompanied him, as they always did whenever he came to the village.

After Millie had searched behind the cabin, even near the outhouse, she waved for Maura to join her. Together, they untied the dogs, which bolted straightaway to the waterfront, drinking heavily for a long time, their brisk lapping like the sound of a moose splashing in the lake. When they had slaked their thirst, they trotted back to the girls, who fed them bits of dried salmon and moose meat they had found in the old man's cache—slowly at first, hoping not to make the starving animals sick from gorging. The dogs were grateful, taking the pieces from the girls' hands.

As Millie and Maura watched them eat, they both felt the only joy they had known in weeks. Tied up as they had been for so long, the dogs could not have eaten the dead. The girls were grateful for these two dogs. They were good dogs, and the sisters decided to take them along, welcoming the companionship of two more survivors of the Great Death. They named the dogs Tundra and Blue, for the one dog, though its fur was black as a moonless winter night, had bright blue eyes.

The canoe glided noiselessly across the far eastern end of the lake toward the mounting current, where the blue-gray river began. A startled fox standing far out on the beach sprinted lightly toward the forest, looking nervously over its shoulder as it ran.

Using her paddle, Millie swung the bow into the lazy current that pulled the canoe downstream. So close to the outlet, the river was slow and wide and deep, and the canoe drifted leisurely at the pace of an unhurried walk.

It required little effort from the girls to keep to the main channel.

Their confidence grew, and they began to think that their entire journey might be so effortless. They wondered why the river was called "swift water." It certainly belied its name. They were content simply to sit and watch as they passed sand and gravel bars, from time to time drawing close to rolling hills where worn game trails came down to the water. Ducks floated on the surface. Geese rested on sandbars. And hungry bears, rummaging along the banks looking for spawned salmon, dashed noiselessly into the forest when the canoe passed by, the dogs barking madly.

There were moments in the first hours that passed with a kind of quiet, restful relief. But even though Millie and Maura tried not to think about their village, the faces of the dead kept rushing back to them.

Around midday they stopped on a sandbar to eat. While the girls made a small campfire, the dogs played in the nearby woods, chasing and barking at squirrels and flushed grouse. Millie took the matches from the tightly sealed jar inside the shovel crate and lit the tinder of dry grass and small twigs, just as her father had taught her. She remembered how he had told her to use paper-birch bark, which burned quickly and easily, and how he said not to smother the flames too soon, adding only a few twigs at a time until the fire grew large enough to breathe on its own. She took out a blackened pot and filled it with water for tea, setting it, teetering, across two stones. While the water rose to a boil, the sisters picked rosehips and blueberries and highbush cranberries from along the riverbank.

They were afraid of venturing too far into the woods.

Tundra brought them a decayed salmon he had found washed ashore. Its soft flesh was white and moldy. It was a putrid gift. But the girls petted him, thanking him for his generosity, even as they tossed it into the river with a stick. The dog waded into the water to retrieve the salmon, but the girls called him back.

When the water was ready, Millie and Maura sat around the smoking fire, feeling its warmth, drinking hot tea, and eating dried salmon, which they shared with the dogs, who stared intently each time either of the girls yanked off a piece with her teeth.

"Why do you think this happened?" Maura asked.

Millie finished chewing her meat. "What do you mean?" she replied.

"Why did everyone get sick and die?"

"I don't know," Millie said simply.

"Why were we spared?" Maura asked.

"I don't know."

Maura appeared to have a whole list of similar unanswerable questions.

"Why did Mother and Father have to die?"

Millie thought of her father, his spotted hands shaking as he patiently showed her how to use the rifle. She thought of her mother convulsing on her thin bed, slipping away in spite of their pleas. She couldn't take any more questions, couldn't take the still-fresh memories.

She said, more harshly than she meant to, "No more questions. I don't have any answers. Perhaps there are none. Some things simply are."

Millie wondered whether she should make up something, some reason why all this was occurring in their lives. She wondered what she might say as she sat avoiding her little sister's eyes.

"Millie?" Maura half whispered.

"What?"

"Are you angry with me?"

Millie finally looked directly at Maura and saw she was crying.

"No, of course not. I just don't know what to say. All I know is that we have to follow the river. We have to find other people who aren't sick."

They sat quietly after that.

Then Maura spoke, slowly and apparently after much thought.

"That's okay. I'll try not to ask so many questions. I wish I could help more. I'm small, but I'm getting bigger."

Millie smiled. "Yes, you are, little sister. Yes, you are."

They packed up after lunch, kicked sand on the smoldering fire. Because the weather was fair, they carefully folded the tarp and lashed it with a short length of rope, stowing it atop the boxes. Maura climbed into the canoe first, and then the dogs leaped aboard and took their positions amid the pile of supplies. When they were ready, Millie shoved off and jumped in, to settle into her place in the stern.

The two sisters were once again on their way.

Konts'aghi

(Seven)

*Raven jumped up and down, he stomped and
stomped, until the overhang avalanched down,
killing all the people below. For the rest of the
winter, he dined on the corpses, savoring the
delicate eyeballs, which were his favorite.*

SOON ENOUGH, THE CURRENT quickened as the river
increased its descent from the high glacial lake. The girls
no longer wondered at its name. Rushing water poured
itself faster through the valley, and the canoe gathered
speed. Both had to work harder and harder to avoid
obstacles, which came at them faster and faster. They
had no time for rest. Several times the canoe almost
smashed into boulders jutting up into the sunlight, the
roiling white waves spraying around them.

"Left!" Millie yelled above the din of the raging river. "Go left!"

And Maura would yell back from the bow, pointing to some approaching object, "Look out!"

The girls paddled so forcefully their arms and shoulders soon sang with pain, but still they fought the water, blinking wetness from their eyes, desperately searching for the next threat. It took all their strength to keep the craft from being swamped. All the while, the dogs tried not to fall out of the canoe as the current twisted it this way and that, dipping into falls and shooting rapids.

Up ahead, on a sharp bend, the girls could see that a bank had given way and a large spruce tree, its roots still holding fast, leaned over the river, some of its branches dragging the surface: a sweeper. The girls paddled frantically, trying to win some distance from the danger, but the current was shoving the little boat straight at the tilted tree. As the canoe passed beneath the drooping boughs, almost sideways, the girls flattened themselves against their supplies.

"Tundra!" Maura shouted.

Millie looked up to see that the dog had been swept into the river. He was bobbing in the raging current, his paws working madly. Canoe and dog were careering together downriver, Tundra drifting farther and farther from the boat. Millie tried to turn the bow downstream, back-paddling to straighten the craft.

"Get ready to grab him!" she yelled once the bow was turned.

For a long, straight stretch the boat and the dog were side by side on the swift river. Maura reached for Tundra and tried to catch hold, but she was not strong enough to grip him to any good effect. He was tiring, the frigid water sapping his strength. His muscles were too cold to do as his brain told them. He was having trouble staying afloat. Maura was crying. It would have been better had the girls left him tied and starving outside the old man's empty cabin. At least there he would have survived the day.

"We have to save him!" Maura shouted. "Get closer!"

She leaned over the canoe as far as she could, and this time she managed to grasp Tundra's scruff and pull him close, holding him tight against the side of the craft with all her strength. His eyes were wide and terrified. Millie crawled over the pile of supplies. Together, the sisters managed to pull the sopping, exhausted dog back into the boat.

No sooner had Millie crawled back to take her place at the stern than the boat struck a submerged boulder. The impact turned the canoe sideways again. Downriver, a series of boulders, like the humps of a dozen giant bears, awaited them. The girls could hear the water rushing around the great stones.

It was thunderous.

Millie looked for a gap big enough for the craft to pass through.

"Right side!" she screamed at Maura. "Paddle hard! Harder!"

Both girls paddled furiously, digging deep, making each stroke count. But the rocks came too fast. The canoe smashed into one of the boulders, which held the craft for only a few seconds, tucking it against stone while the river poured itself into the canoe, swamping it. The dogs jumped out as the supplies were lifted out of the boat to swirl around the boulder, the chests and the tarp and the dried bundles of salmon, all spinning together, held fast by the foaming eddy.

The screaming girls gripped the gunwales of the canoe. But when the gushing water had entirely filled it, the boat sank, taking Maura's small game rifle with it, and the girls and the dogs were swept downriver amid the flotsam of their provisions.

Unable to swim, Maura could only try to stay atop the current. As Blue swept by, she managed to grab hold of him. But the skinny sled dog was not buoyant enough to keep them both afloat. Dog and girl went under. Millie swam to her sister and grabbed her around the neck, holding her head above water, as the current tossed and twisted them remorselessly. She looked for a safe place toward which to swim.

Tundra was already standing on a gravel bar, shaking himself dry. Blue and Millie, hauling Maura, who continued to struggle, swam as hard as they could. The river's iciness was already taking effect, so piercing even their bones ached.

This far north and this late in the season, it didn't take long for the cold to steal every last ounce of body heat, stiffening muscles.

Finally, Blue and both girls managed to reach the shallows about a hundred yards downriver from where Tundra had landed. They waded ashore, drenched, holding on to each other, trembling. Blue clambered onto the beach, shaking the river from his fur, spraying a rain of droplets over the dry pebbles, turning them dark.

Tundra ran to greet them, dripping a long, thin, shining line in the sunlight.

The girls looked downstream just in time to see the two chests disappear around the bend. Perhaps they could salvage them. Though shivering and sopping wet, their clothes heavy as chains, Millie and Maura ran along the shore after the crates. The dogs followed. The running warmed them.

They caught sight of the steamer trunk as it vanished again far ahead of them at the next sharp curve. They did not see the other chest and assumed that it too was gone. The sisters stood on the wide shore, defeated. The oblivious dogs wandered through a thicket of leafless willows, snuffling the vague scent of rabbits or grouse.

Something downstream caught Maura's attention. She stepped closer to see what it was.

"Look! The other box!" she yelled, pointing.

Millie saw it, too. The long rectangular crate had not been carried away by the current but had been drawn into an eddy, wedged against a logjam. The sisters ran to it, plunged knee-deep into the icy water, and dragged the wooden box ashore. They opened the lid. Inside was the pile of folded blankets, their winter clothing, the cooking pot they had used to boil tea, the waterproof jar of matches, their father's rifle, a box of cartridges, a knife, a hatchet, and a coil of rope. Only a little water had seeped into the box.

As they stood celebrating their good fortune, the folded tarp floated by close to the riverbank. It must have been caught by a sweeper or back-eddy. Millie trudged into the water and grabbed the rope-tied bundle as it passed. It was waterlogged and heavy.

Maura helped her pull it out beside the open crate.

Shaking from the cold, the sisters untied the tarp, unfolded it, and draped it across a stand of willows to dry. They built a small fire beneath it, took off their wet clothes, and hung them on sticks close to the flames. They sat together on a weathered log, huddled under a blanket. When their clothes were dry, the girls collected enough firewood to last the night and picked handfuls of overripe berries for supper. There was nothing else to eat. The bundles of dried salmon were lost, returned to the river.

The sisters had survived again. They had lost the

steamer trunk, which contained extra clothes, the frying pan, traps and snares, the candles, and other important equipment. They had even lost the long-handled ax and a shovel. But though they had no canoe and few provisions, they still had hope—the steadfast resolve of those who have nothing else.

That night, as green ribbons of northern lights arched across the sky, the girls and the dogs slept, exhausted, close to the fire, which snapped and popped and hissed in the darkness—the thieving river sliding beyond the yellow dim light.

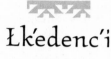

Łk'edenc'i

(Eight)

*Then, in the spring, Raven flew away to look
for someone else to deceive. He was hungry
again. He saw a woman with three young boys
walking along a woodland trail. She was poor
and hungry and filthy. Her children were sick
and starving.*

A WET, SLUSHY SNOW was falling the next morning,
turning the hills and trees in the valley silvery-white
below a steel-gray sky. Although it was a wet snow,
which would not outlast the morning, the girls were dry
beneath the tarp draped over the low willows.

Far off in the hills, a lonesome wolf howled.

The howling awakened Millie, who slowly opened
her eyes, resentful that she had been stirred from a

dream. She crawled out from the tarp's shelter and stood up, the heavy red blanket hanging from her hunched shoulders like a shawl. Her muscles were stiff from sleeping on the hard ground, her ears and nose cold. As she looked at the cool, gray ghost of the fire, she suddenly realized that the spot across from her, where her sister had fallen asleep, was vacant. Maura's blanket was lying across the weathered log. The dogs were also gone.

The faraway wolf howled again.

Millie felt the grip of a nauseating fear. She wondered if wolves had taken her sister. She had failed to keep her promise to watch over Maura. The white snow was settling lightly onto Millie's bright red blanket and her long black hair.

"Maura," she said, so softly that even *she* couldn't hear the word above the din of the river.

She turned slowly, looking in every direction for her sister, for a sign.

"Maura!" she screamed.

The loud river didn't answer. The silent hills didn't answer. And the spruce trees only swayed in the slight breeze blowing the snow sideways.

Millie shouted her sister's name again and waited.

Nothing. She cupped her hands around her mouth and shouted yet again. She heard a sound approaching from upriver. But the sound was not Maura, only a low-flying duck. Its beating wings propelled it to the distant bend, and it was gone.

Millie ran downriver, still clutching the blanket under her chin for warmth. She did not see her sister or the dogs. The notion crept into her mind that she might face the rest of the journey alone, might face the rest of her life alone. She felt her heartbeat quicken, a fluttering like a flock of small birds.

She turned and walked briskly back toward the makeshift camp, shivering, her eyes beginning to fill with tears.

"M-a-u-r-a!" she yelled, her voice breaking as she began to cry. "Maura!"

When she reached camp, she crawled beneath the tarp and built a small fire. She sat beside it staring into it as if the flames were meaningful, as if they held her future. The flickering fire and the curling smoke reminded her of the burned bodies back in the village. She wondered if she might be the very last person in the world.

Lost in her grieving, Millie did not hear Tundra approach, did not immediately sense his presence. And then, startled, she snapped her head to see Tundra sitting beside her. She looked up and there was Maura emerging from the woods, Blue following happily at her side.

Millie crawled out from beneath the tarp and jumped to her feet.

"Maura! Where have you been? I . . . I . . ."

But her words were hushed by the sound of the river.

Maura did not hear her until she was standing alongside the tarp.

"Where have you been?" asked Millie, inconspicuously wiping away a tear, trying to hide that she had been crying.

"I woke up early," Maura replied. "I was hungry, so I went and picked berries." She showed Millie a pocket full of assorted berries.

Millie straightened her dress with her hands. She cleared her throat before she spoke. "I thought the wolves got you," she said sternly. "Next time tell me before you do something like that."

Maura sat down on the log and pulled handfuls of berries from her pockets.

"I'm sorry. I didn't want to wake you up. You looked so peaceful in your blanket. Want some?" she asked, holding out a cupped hand.

For the next hour the girls sat quietly beneath the tarp beside the campfire eating, occasionally petting a dog whenever one came near. Maura had fed them palmfuls of berries in the woods. They wanted more. As they sat Millie and Maura thought about the people in their village and about the long, uncertain journey ahead. They both worried, yet neither said a word, trying to be strong for the other.

Little by little, the snowfall slowed and turned into a rainy drizzle, and the whiteness was washed from the land.

Before long, the rain stopped, the sky cleared somewhat, and while the midday sun warmed the northern world, the sisters readied themselves for their trek downriver. They had no idea how far they would eventually have to walk to find other people, but they understood that without the canoe the rest of their travels would be on foot.

They planned.

The crate they had salvaged from the river was too

heavy to carry by hand, even with the two of them, along the narrow, brush-covered, and often vanishing trail. So they decided to share the burden in what seemed a more efficient way, dividing the supplies. Millie carried more weight since she was older and stronger.

Maura cut a length of rope and tied it around her waist as a kind of belt, hanging the hatchet on one side and the leather-sheathed hunting knife on the other. When Millie turned around and saw her sister garbed in her blanket-shawl, cinched at the waist with her rope belt and its attached hardware, she was a little shocked. Maura looked quite fierce. She had also rolled up the blankets with the parkas and mukluks in the middle, tied the bundles securely, and fashioned a kind of rope harness, which she slung over her shoulders. The burden was bulky but relatively light.

Millie draped the coiled rope over one shoulder and folded the heavy canvas tarp with the pot and jar of matches tucked safely inside. She was able to wear the tarp like a rucksack, holding the loops of the rope with both hands. The girls divided the remaining bullets, placing them into pockets, lessening the chance of losing all of them at once.

The brass cartridges clinked as they walked about.

When they were packed, Millie grabbed the rifle from where it was leaning against the weathered log and set out resolutely down the trail, with Maura close behind her. The dogs wandered ahead, exploring every scent along the way. Sunlight danced on the ground through spruce boughs, and low clouds tangled in the hilltops, bending to the blue-gray curve of the sky.

For the most part, the forest trail, faintly blazed by hatchet marks on tree trunks, followed the river only a few steps from the bank. But every now and then, it opened onto long gravel bars and the girls would see bear tracks in the sand and mud, some very large. At such times, Millie would hold the loaded rifle a little more firmly, concerned that they might come upon a startled, unwary bear.

At least they had the dogs. Their keen noses would smell bears from a long way off. Twice the dogs began barking and bolted into the forest, only to emerge later with their tails wagging. Perhaps, the girls thought, they had merely smelled a grouse or a rabbit or a moose.

In the late afternoon, the dogs raced down the trail and began barking madly. Millie nervously checked the rifle chamber, certain that they were tangling with a bear. They walked slowly, Maura staying behind her sister. Millie held her breath as she approached the ruckus, her hands trembling, the shaking rifle aimed toward the noise. But it was only a porcupine, standing still with its rump turned to the dogs. Blue's snout was full of quills, which served only to increase his ferocity toward the motionless creature.

It was the way of all dogs, a kind of innate, endearing stupidity. Millie had seen her father and uncles pull quills from dogs only to watch them rush right back for more.

The girls knew how to kill and clean porcupine. They had helped their father and their uncles. They liked its dark meat, especially boiled into its own soup. There was no need to waste a bullet. Aside from the sharp quills, which porcupines do not throw or shoot at attackers, despite the myths, the creature was defenseless. A simple clubbing would kill it almost instantly. It had no protection against the club.

Millie found a stout stick, and while Maura pulled the two barking dogs away, Millie clubbed its head. It took three tries, but she killed it. There are no quills on a porcupine's feet, so she rolled it over with the stick and pulled it by a leg. She dragged it down to the river's edge.

The dogs cautiously sniffed at it and growled before joining the sisters as they gathered kindling and firewood. Most of the wood on the ground was soaked from the morning's wet snow and drizzle, but they were able to gather great armfuls of dry twigs and branches from the undergrowth of spruce trees. The upper boughs had concealed them from even a hard rain. They built a large fire, and when it was ready, Millie rolled the porcupine onto the flames, turning it with a stick until all the quills had burned away. With the quills gone, it is as easy to quarter a porcupine as it is to quarter a rabbit or beaver.

While Millie cut up supper, Maura carefully pulled quills from Blue's swollen snout. It was a difficult task. The dog flinched and whimpered and tried to wriggle free, but he understood what the girl was doing and did not bite. No doubt he had encountered porcupines before. He tried to be brave. Tundra lay near the fire, watching the commotion. Using a trick learned from her father, Maura used two flat skipping stones to grip each dark brown-and-white needlelike quill, pulling fast and hard until all the quills were gone.

Blue licked her face when she was done and then ran off to play with Tundra along the river.

Millie roasted some of the meat on sticks; some she tossed into a pot of boiling water. She cooked the entire porcupine, giving the dogs a fair share. After all, it was they who had cornered it. There was enough cooked meat to last for several days, especially now that the weather was turning colder and the meat would not spoil quickly.

While Millie tended to the boiling soup, stirring it with a twig, Maura sat on a boulder, whittling bark from a stout stick, making herself a walking cane, which came up to her shoulders. Listening to the river, Maura thought of Mother and Father and of all the dead people back in their village. She couldn't forget their faces, the burned bodies, the scavenging dogs and bears, the smell. She tried to put the images out of her mind. It all seemed far away and unreal, even though they really hadn't traveled so far.

Since it was already late in the evening, the sun resting on the lip of hills, the sisters made camp. For the rest of the night, the four travelers sat around a warming fire, eating porcupine, drinking the rich meaty broth, and watching constellations move across the sky—the slow dance of the galaxy spinning around the North Star.

Ts'iłk'ey Kole
(Nine)

Raven flew down and landed on a tree.

"Why are you traveling all alone?" he asked the destitute woman. "Where are your people? Where is your husband?"

The woman was frightened. She had never seen a talking raven before.

The next afternoon, as the girls marched along the leaf-blanketed trail carrying their cumbersome packs—Maura singing one of her favorite songs to console herself—a cow moose and her calf sprang up without warning. The cow almost trampled the girls, who had surprised her sleeping in an alder thicket just off the path. The dogs, chasing sandpipers and seagulls along the riverbank, had not smelled the moose—the wind was blowing from the wrong direction.

The two moose trotted onto the gravel shoreline. The dogs saw them and abruptly burst after them, barking as they ran. To escape, the cow plunged into the choppy water and swam toward the other bank, as the treacherous current carried her far downriver. The dogs followed on the gravel bank, barking continually. But she was strong and heavy. She made it to the other side.

The little calf, unnoticed by the dogs, was left behind, uncertain of following her mother into the raging river. She called to her mother while stepping hesitantly into the water up to her belly. The current snatched her and dragged her downriver. She was too small and too young to fight the roiling waters, which tossed her about and rolled her head-over-hoof. She was drowning. Her feebleminded mother stood on the far shore watching.

"We have to save it!" Maura yelled to her sister, as she ran along the gravel bar, trying to catch up with the drowning moose calf. When she was just ahead of it at a spot that looked to be less swift and less deep, Maura dropped her pack of blankets on the gravel beach and crashed nearly up to her waist into the river.

Millie tried to catch up, but her heavy, bulky load slowed her.

"Stop, Maura!" she yelled. "You can't swim! You'll drown!"

Although Maura weighed less than the calf, she caught hold of it just long enough for it to regain a foothold and stand upright in the shallow water. When the half-drowned calf was standing safely on shore, Maura trudged back to her sister, smiling broadly, the soaking-wet dress and blanket-shawl clinging to her skinny body.

Tundra and Blue were still far down the gravel bar, barking at the cow moose standing on the opposite bank.

"Are you crazy?" Millie asked.

"I had to save it," Maura replied, shivering from the icy water, her arms wrapped across her chest. "We scared it into the river. It would have been our fault if it had died. I couldn't save anyone in the village. . . . I *had* to save the moose. It was our fault, don't you see?"

Millie was looking intently in the opposite direction, at something over Maura's shoulder. The baby moose was approaching. Maura turned slowly and saw the calf. When it stopped, only a few steps from her, Maura held out her open hand. The calf jumped sideways, as if to turn and flee, but it did not run away. The two girls remained very still. Again the calf moved forward. It walked right up to Maura and sniffed her hand. Both girls barely breathed. And then the calf stepped closer and pressed its blond head against Maura's waist and held it there while Maura stroked its cheeks and long nose, speaking to it softly.

"*Kasuun deniigi.* Beautiful little moose," she whispered.

The dumbstruck cow stood across the river, watching safely from her side of nature, blinking, unable to fathom the moment.

Millie also stood quietly. She had never seen or heard of anything like this. Her eyes filled with warm tears. She too touched the calf, ran her fingers gently through its soft mane and smelled the musty odor of its wet coat. And then the calf bolted lightly back to the water's edge.

The girls walked downriver to fetch the dogs, who were still barking at the cow moose on the other side of the water. Then they returned to the forest trail, holding the dogs to keep them from harassing the calf, watching from afar as the anxious cow finally swam back across the churning river, rejoined her calf, and vanished into the trees, the calf at her heels.

When they were far enough away, Millie built a large fire to warm and dry her sister. They ate roasted porcupine. Though Millie was angry that her sister had risked her life so foolishly, she was also proud of her. While she sat by the fire, poking a stick at the embers, she couldn't help but wonder what she would have done if Maura had drowned saving the calf.

Maura was all that she had in the world.

Later that same day, about two miles downriver from where Maura had saved the moose calf, the girls saw something curious in the water. Their trail was meandering along a hillside, perhaps a hundred feet from the shore and about ten feet in elevation above the river, so at first they didn't recognize what it was. They picked their way through the brush and down the slope, until they were close enough to see that it was a human body, as pale as ghosts in stories the sisters recalled the elders telling. The People believed that spirits of the dead roam the natural world, oblivious to the fact that they are dead. Even the spirits of animals walk the earth, doing the same things they had done in life, for the most part invisible to the living.

The torso was submerged just below the surface, caught on a log, bent over backward, the face staring at the sky.

And though the corpse was swollen and discolored, translucent as the soft, white flesh of grayling or whitefish, the girls could tell that it was the man from the empty cabin upriver where they had found Tundra and Blue.

The old man's dogs now stood on the high bank beside the two sisters, sniffing the air uneasily, whining softly as they looked down at the pale and grotesque face of their dead owner.

Millie was the first to speak. "He must have come downriver just as we have." They figured that the man wandered off in a fevered delirium caused by the red spots and fell into the river, his mottled body carried by the current, eventually lodging against this log.

"Should we bury him?" Maura asked without taking her eyes off the pale cadaver, one lazy arm floating up and down as if waving good-bye.

Millie agreed that it would be the right thing to do, but first they would have to retrieve his body.

The cut bank was deep, and swift water pressed the man against the log. Neither sister could see a way to wade out there. Finding a long stick, Millie tried to hook the ragged clothing still cloaking much of the corpse. They took turns, but were unable to catch anything.

Millie decided what they needed was a longer pole and something more hooklike; so she affixed a sharply curved, foot-long piece of wood to the end of the stick with a length of rope.

She tried again, this time dropping the hooked end of the pole slightly upstream of the man, allowing the current to wash it downriver, snagging the waving arm.

"Pull," grunted Millie, already tugging with all her weight.

Maura helped heave, and together they managed to free the body from the log. But the deadweight was too heavy in the strong current. It broke loose and floated away. Frustrated, the girls watched as the body was carried downriver, sinking slowly into the shadowy depths until there was nothing left to see except the river and the foaming boulders and the rising moon, perfectly nestled between two ridges in the darkening valley.

The sisters made camp on a sandbar, setting up the tarp like a tent over a long pole. They built a crackling fire outside the tent and sat beside it while the dogs licked and scratched themselves. Neither sister said a word, even when both crawled into their bedding, closed their eyes, and tried not to think about corpses adrift on blue water as they lay close by the fire, which eventually burned down to a heap of cold ashes, as cold and gray as the ash mounds in their abandoned village.

And while they waited for sleep, snow fell as lightly as ash, as silently as ash, unmelting. This would be the night of ashes.

Hwlazaan

(Ten)

"My husband died in a hunting accident," she replied, her voice trembling in fear. "I have been outcast to wander the wilderness with my three small boys. We are cold and hungry and lost, and I fear that we will not survive long."

THE TARP SAGGED so low from the night's snowfall that Maura couldn't even sit upright without her head touching it. She pushed aside the door flap, which was no more than two ends of the tarp brought together and held in place by stones. Almost a foot of snow lay on the ground, dead-white and pillowed, the load bending double the thin willows and alders. The heavy snow muffled even the silence.

The low sun was as pale as a seagull egg or a river stone.

Maura sighed as she retreated to her sleeping place, her body searching for the warmth left there. She could see her breath, and her hands were already cold. Winter had come to stay. It would not leave again until spring, six months away. The rest of their journey would be hard going, slower, less certain. From now on there would be thin ice, overflow, snowdrifts and blizzards, and worst of all, occasional days of punishing cold.

Although neither girl had spoken and Millie had not moved, Maura knew that her sister was awake. "Millie, do we have enough clothes to keep us warm when the winter really sets in?"

Millie turned over, toward her sister. "I think so. At least we don't have to carry the mukluks and parkas. We can wear them. I'm sure we can stay warm during the day while we're walking. Nighttime will be the hard part."

"We'll have to sleep in our parkas, won't we?" Maura was imagining how it would feel to sleep with no cabin, no roof, no protection but a tarp above them in the knife-edge cold of winter.

"And we'll have to keep a fire going," Millie answered.

"We'll have to be sure to tend the fire." She wanted to sound confident for her little sister, but she, too, imagined the coming cold, the deeper snow, the freezing of the world.

As the morning sun struggled above the rim of the hills, Maura got up and built a small fire with the remaining pieces of dry spruce. While the inside of the drooping makeshift tent warmed, the girls ate what remained of the roasted porcupine, which wasn't much. A few small bites each. The dogs stared and drooled and begged, but there wasn't enough to share with them. The meager portions did not even lessen the girls' hunger.

Millie and Maura thought about food as they put on their winter clothing and packed camp, shaking snow from the tarp before folding it. They hoped to kill another porcupine soon. The dogs searched the nearby woods, perhaps similarly hoping to corner one again.

Although the northland was now buried in winter, the graveled edge of the river was exposed. Delicate sheets of paper-thin ice formed like spiderwebs along the water's edge. As winter temperatures drop, glaciers stop melting, and lakes and rivers and creeks dry up, retreating into their deepest beds to reveal ever-widening shorelines. In another week, a person would be able to walk across the river in most places.

As they trod slowly and carefully along the exposed-gravel shore, Millie was first to see a flock of grouse near a steep bank, searching for small round pebbles. Grouse are about the same size as chickens, which explains why many old-timers call them spruce chickens. They commonly come down to river and creek beds in the morning to swallow tiny stones. The stones go into a pouch called a gizzard and help the birds to grind leaves and berries and digest them.

"Sssshhh," Millie whispered as she stopped walking and pointed at the flock.

The dogs, trailing behind, hadn't noticed the birds yet.

Then Maura, with her walking stick in hand, saw the oblivious grouse pecking at the gravel. The girls knew the birds were not the wariest or smartest of wild creatures. They had seen village boys kill them by throwing stones.

"You hold the dogs, and I'll try to kill one," Millie

whispered, slowly pulling the heavy tarp pack from her shoulders. She set the rifle aside, across the pack. The big gun was designed to kill moose or caribou or bear, and Millie knew that in the unlikely event that she actually hit a bird with a shot, nothing would be left to eat. She wished that they had not lost the other rifle, which was more suitable for small game.

But it lay uselessly rusting on the bottom of the river.

While Millie crept toward the birds, crouching, careful not to make any noise, Maura knelt and held the dogs, speaking to them softly, calming them. When Millie was close, she picked up two stones. She hurled the first one at the middle of the flock, just missing one bird, which hopped a little in surprise. But the rest only looked up from their pecking, saw nothing of importance, and went back to gathering pebbles.

The dogs saw the birds now, and they began to whimper and twitch. They wanted to chase the grouse, watch them explode into the air when they were almost in their midst. They often did the same thing to seagulls on the beach below the village. They never actually caught a bird. It was just a dog game.

Millie aimed and hurled the second rock, which hit the ground in front of the closest bird, throwing up a little blast of sand. The bird took flight. The rest followed. And Millie and Maura and the dogs watched as the whole flock flew over the treetops, banked sharply, and vanished into the forest.

There would be no roasted grouse for lunch. Everyone's stomach grumbled. Maura swallowed her impulse to blame her sister for missing the bird, and Millie held back her frustration and self-contempt. How did the boys kill grouse that way? The dogs hungrily sniffed the ground where the birds had been.

Later that afternoon, the girls approached a stretch of river where the water level had dropped so suddenly that several trout had been stranded in a shallow pool, unable to make it back to the channel. It was easy for the girls to build a weir by placing rocks across one end of the pool, trapping the fish in a smaller area. Then they simply used Maura's walking stick to flip them out of the water onto the gravel flat.

While Maura gathered firewood, Millie cleaned the fish with her sister's knife. For a long time the gutted fish twitched on the bloodstained stones. Maura suddenly stopped and turned toward the forest. A cold chill seized her.

"Millie," she said tensely, holding the bundle of dry wood in her arms, "do you think bears will come for these fish?"

Millie continued cleaning the fish, flinging their entrails into the river.

"It's too late for bears," she said. "They've likely all gone in search of dens."

She knew how smart bears are. And not only bears. Most birds abandon the northland before the snows. Beavers rarely come out from their mud-and-stick houses, and squirrels leave their nests only to retrieve seeds they collected all summer. Only the most unfortunate creatures, moose and caribou, wolf and man, dwell on the frozen land, hardship a constant companion.

The dogs kept trying to steal fish whenever the girls weren't looking. But because there were enough, Millie let them each have one. Blue carried his fish into the woods to eat. Tundra took his downriver a ways. After Millie had cleaned the rest, the girls roasted them on willow sticks over a fire. They ate nearly everything, including the blackened skin and the crunchy tails, a favorite. Only the largest bones were left.

With their stomachs filled, despair seemed a little farther away.

That evening, with an hour of sunlight remaining and the first stars beginning to show, Millie and Maura were startled by an old man. As they were walking on the trail high above where the river had cut a deep channel against the bank, snow crunching underfoot, they saw him standing about a hundred yards ahead of them. From where they were, Maura thought he looked like the drowned man they had tried to pull from the river the day before.

Millie began to shout and wave, trying to catch his attention. Maura joined in.

"Hello!" they called, happy that they would not be alone any longer. "Hello!"

The dogs, seeing the man, bolted down the trail barking, kicking up snow as they ran.

The girls yelled at them to come back.

"Tundra! Blue! Come here!"

Maura even whistled, the way her father had taught

her, forcing breath between curled tongue and tightened lips.

But the dogs either did not hear or did not care to stop. The girls ran after them, though not nearly as fast. The bullets in their pockets clinked with their steps. When the dogs had covered a little over half the distance, the man suddenly turned and fled down the steep bank toward the river. With surprising agility he raced to a slender stretch of gravel bar. Millie and Maura couldn't see him as they continued along the tree-lined trail, but they could hear the dogs barking.

After making their way down the rocky, root-tangled embankment, the girls came out on the gravel shoreline and there saw the dogs barking at the man, who was now standing on the other side of the river. Each sister grabbed a dog to hold and quiet.

"Hello! Don't be afraid!" Millie shouted, cupping her hands around her mouth so that her words would carry over the rushing water. "The dogs are friendly!"

The man did not respond. He stared blankly.

"Can you help us?" Millie shouted. "Please come back!"

Millie was about to shout again, but Maura clutched her sister's arm and hushed her. It was then that Millie noticed that the man was not wet. She looked up and down the river. She could see no place he could have crossed without getting drenched.

The current was deep and fast. No one could have swum across here. It was impossible.

Suddenly, the man flew into the air and perched atop a tall spruce tree. He stood on the very tip-top of the tree, swaying, looking down at the girls and at the dogs, which were barking wildly. He seemed to be frightened. Then he ran away, his feet barely touching the tops of trees as he fled through the air.

The girls never saw him again.

When they started to climb back to the main trail, retracing their route up the steep snow-covered path, they noticed that the only footprints in the snow were the dogs' and their own. For the rest of the night, they tried to convince themselves of what they had seen. They had heard stories told by elders of how spirits are unaware that they are dead. Elders say that if you touch such a ghost the spirit will fall instantly back into his or her body, wherever it is, and come alive again.

At least that is what they say.

Seeing the ghost made Millie and Maura wonder about all the dead people back in their village. Were their spirits floating through the empty houses? Were Mother and Father among them? And if so, were they looking for their daughters?

Ts'iłk'ey Uk'edi

(Eleven)

For the first time, Raven did not think about his hunger. For the first time, he did not feel like deceiving someone. He pitied the poor woman's plight. He actually felt sorry for her and her starving children.

"I will help you," he said.

IT DID NOT SNOW for the next two days, yet it was cold enough that the river began to freeze. Sheets of ice spanned the slowest places. Sometimes the river never froze where the water was fast and deep. In such stretches vapor would rise from the open water, a sure sign of danger.

Maura stopped and planted the end of her walking stick firmly beside her. She raised her head, turning it slowly, sniffing the air.

"Do you smell that?" she asked finally, turning to look at her sister.

Millie also sniffed the wind. "Smoke," she said, smiling.

The dogs had smelled the smoke for a long time but had given no sign of interest or of fear.

Millie and Maura were aware that lightning strikes, which caused wildfires in summer, held no power in the frozen wetness of winter. The scent of smoke could only mean that someone was nearby, downriver, since the gentle breeze came from that direction. They hoped it was the village they had been searching for, the one Father had said was halfway to the white settlement where the two rivers came together, the one where the man who had guided the two white men had come from.

They walked faster. It was already dusk, darkness beginning to push away the light. The girls hoped to find the village before nightfall.

As they strode around a long bend, they saw a log cabin on the other side of the river. Smoke rose from the roof, and a warm yellow light glowed through a window. This entire stretch of river had frozen over. Maura held the dogs as Millie shuffled across first, stopping frequently to listen to the ice, which occasionally popped and sent splinter lines across the smooth surface. In the near darkness, she could see the humps of great rocks beneath her. The ice wasn't yet thick. But if it supported her weight, she thought, it would surely support her little sister.

When Millie was standing on the far shore, she gestured that it was safe to cross. Maura released Tundra and Blue, who ran over the frozen river without concern. Neither dog weighed more than fifty or sixty pounds. Maura shuffled across slowly, but she eventually made it safely to the other side.

They approached the small cabin. A moose hide was stretched between two trees, and two quarters of moose meat were hung from a pole. A log lay between sawhorses beside a stump with an ax stuck in it.

Millie knocked on the door.

At first they heard only the sound of movement: rustling and heavy boots on rough boards. The door opened a crack and then, suddenly, wider. A giant of a man stood in the doorway. He was taller than the girls' father by a foot, and thickly built. His face was hidden within a great beard, concealing every facial feature except the narrow bridge of his nose and his deep-set eyes. The girls could see no mouth. Even his eyebrows were bushy. Bright red suspenders held his pants up.

Both girls immediately recalled the scary stories elders told about Bush Indians, wild animal-like men who dwelt in the forest, their bodies covered in fur, bear-like. Parents often warned children not to wander too far into the woods lest Bush Indians snatch them.

The grizzled man was wary at first, but then only surprised. He was not accustomed to having visitors, being one of those hardy men who stayed in the north at the end of the Gold Rush, more content to live alone in the wilderness than among people, only occasionally rejoining civilization to trade furs or gold for needed provisions.

When he saw that his guests could mean him no harm and were not thieves, like the bears who some-times made off with his curing meat, he broke into laughter.

"Why, you're but little girls. Welcome!" said the giant as he ushered the girls inside, kicking Tundra when he tried to follow.

"Out!" he shouted, and closed the door firmly. Millie

and Maura did not understand the word, but they understood the act.

The girls noticed a narrow bed built against the back wall, a small table, a chair, cans and tins and boxes and bottles on shelves, a rifle leaning in a corner, rusted traps and furs hanging on the walls, a pot and a black frying pan suspended from the ceiling. In many ways the cabin was like their home back in the village. But instead of a fire pit, the heat came from a heavy-looking rectangular metal box, which stood on short legs. A pot of beans sat on top of the heated box.

"My goodness, what are you girls doing out there alone? How far have you come?" the man asked.

The girls smiled dumbly. They were cold. They did not understand a single word he said.

"Where are your families?" the man said slowly. "Where did you come from?"

The girls could only stare and smile and embrace the warm air with its smell of smoke and beans and unwashed clothing.

Millie asked if they could stay and warm up for a while. She asked if they were near a village. She said she and her sister were hungry.

Now the great, bearded man looked blank and foolish. He did not understand Millie's words any more than she had understood his. But he could see that the girls were cold, and he could see the way their eyes kept bouncing back to the pot of beans. He gently took the rifle from Millie and leaned it against the wall beside the door. He gestured for the girls to take off their packs and to sit by the warm stove. Millie sat on the chair; Maura stood beside her.

The man jumped to the door, opened it, and then seized a log from his woodpile along with an armful of split firewood. As he stepped back inside, he kicked the door closed with a practiced foot. After positioning the short log alongside Millie's chair and nodding for Maura to sit, he opened the door on the metal box, shoved a piece of wood inside, poked at it with a stick, and then closed the clanking door. The fire began to roar, and soon the metal sides glowed softly red.

While the girls warmed, the man went outside and returned with a chunk of moose meat, which he cut into thick pieces and stirred into the pot of beans. He added salt and what seemed to the girls to be black specks from a boxed shaker. The soup smelled good. Millie and

Maura were very hungry. They had not eaten since consuming the last pieces of trout that morning.

When the beans and meat were cooked, the man filled three bowls, setting two on the table, with two metal spoons, before the famished girls.

"Soup," he said, pointing to the bowls. "Soup. Eat up."

The man took his bowl and sat on the edge of his bed. He blew across each spoonful of the near-boiling broth and then sipped and slurped the soup. The girls watched him take a bite of the meat. That was enough for them. They eagerly ate their portions, blowing and slurping each hot spoonful. They were happy for the food. The man began to laugh, showing his dark-colored teeth, and soon all three diners were laughing in unison. Between mouthfuls, the man spoke to the girls, smiling, though it was hard to tell because his unkempt mustache covered his mouth.

"I reckon you girls are from that village upriver," he said aloud. He had noted the direction of their footprints in the snow when he was outside gathering firewood from the woodpile.

"I haven't been up that way in years. But I reckon I

know your father. I know most of the Indian men between here and the big glacier. I wonder what brings you girls downriver all by yourself during early winter."

Millie and Maura continued eating, listening to the kind man who had offered them his hospitality and warm food. Nothing the man said made any sense to them, but Millie was certain that it was the same language the men who brought the box with legs had spoken.

After supper, the man pulled out a slender metallic device, which fit easily in the palms of his hands. He smiled and then raised it to his mouth and blew. Suddenly, the small room filled with music, startling the girls. But they quickly calmed down and listened. They liked the sounds. They giggled at the funny expressions on the man's face, his cheeks puffing out and in as he breathed into his hands.

When it was time for bed, the man took the bedrolls from Maura's pack and unrolled them on the floor. He patted the floor and made a gesture to mean sleeping. The girls understood. Besides, it was late, and they were tired from walking since first light. Before crawling into their blankets, Millie and Maura stepped outside to relieve themselves in the outhouse. They gave Blue and

Tundra each a small bowl of beans and meat, which the dogs ate quickly, licking the bowls clean.

Shortly thereafter, the man was fast asleep in his narrow bed, snoring loudly. Despite the incessant noise, both girls fell asleep quickly, grateful for the stove's rattling warmth, for the man's kindness, and for their good fortune.

Millie and Maura awoke to the warmth of the cabin and the smell of brewed coffee. They could hear noise outside. Millie stood up and looked out the small window. The giant, hairy-faced man was sawing the log between the sawhorses. There was a pile of short logs on the ground, which he had already cut with a red-handled saw. They looked to be the right length to fit inside the woodstove. The dogs lay on the ground watching the man. They had seen men cut wood before.

The girls rolled up their bedding and tied it into a bundle as they had done every morning since leaving their village. Millie set it atop the folded tarp lying beside the door, her rifle leaning against the wall behind it.

The rest of the pot of beans and meat sat beside the coffeepot on the stove. The beans had cooked down until they were no longer soupy but thick and pasty. Two clean bowls and spoons sat on the table. Maura partially filled the bowls and sat on the log the man had brought in as a chair the night before. Millie sat on the chair again. They ate their breakfast and shared a cup of coffee. They did not like its bitterness. Millie poured the rest of the cup back into the coffeepot.

They drank cold water instead.

"We sure are lucky to have found such a nice man to help us," said Maura, looking around the warm cabin.

"Yes," replied Millie. "Raven must be helping us."

But both girls knew that Raven rarely did anything nice for anyone. He was a selfish and greedy trickster who enjoyed causing suffering above all else. He reveled in deception.

"I like it here," said Maura, spooning out a piece of moose meat from her beans. "It's near the river, for fish, and there must be plenty of game. And his cabin is sheltered from storms."

"We can't stay here," answered her sister. "He isn't of our people. We have to continue downriver."

"Oh, Millie. Can't we stay at least for a while? We can work for him. We can make him mukluks and mend his clothes."

"He's a white man, Maura. We don't know his ways, and he doesn't know ours. We have to find the village. It must be nearby, just a little farther downriver."

For some moments Maura thought about this. "Perhaps he will guide us. I would be glad for that," she said, smiling.

Millie stood up and looked out the window. The man was rolling a large stump close to the pile of sawed logs. When it was in position, he set a log on the stump and cleaved it in half with a single powerful swing of his ax.

"I'll try to ask him. I don't know how, but I'll try," Millie finally replied, and then she sat down to finish her breakfast.

When they were done eating, the girls went outside to clean their bowls and spoons using handfuls of snow. The day was gray and cold and windless. After cleaning the dishes, the sisters helped the man. Millie set logs on the stump for him to split in half; Maura stacked them neatly on top of the woodpile against the cabin. When that chore was finished, he showed them how to fetch water from an open hole he maintained in the river ice. He also set a fishing line in the hole, using bits of moose liver as bait.

Several times Millie tried to speak to the man.

"Can you tell me how close we are to the village downriver? Can you take us there?" she asked in her language. She even pointed downriver and used her hands and fingers to gesture walking.

But the man didn't understand. He nodded his head and walked away.

Around midday, the man put on his heavy boots and winter coat and then took up his rifle. The sisters looked at him questioningly, fearful that he was leaving them. He grabbed hold of a trap and rattled it. The girls understood that he was going to check his traps.

While he was away, Millie and Maura heated water on the stove and washed themselves for the first time since leaving home. It had been their custom to take steam baths twice a week. Every village had a small structure built just for that purpose. Indeed, the names in their language for two days of the week were directly related to the ritual of bathing. Men and boys always went first, then women and girls, who had to fetch their own firewood and water.

Maura had brought a comb from home. It had been her mother's. She kept it tucked inside her parka. It was the one small comfort she carried with her, a reminder of happier times, of all the nights her mother used to comb out her long black hair while humming softly. The sisters took turns combing tangles from each other's hair.

As Millie was working on Maura's hair, Maura whispered, "Remember how Mother liked to comb our hair, then spread it out in her hands?"

"Yes, of course," replied Millie. "Remember how she always hummed some tune?"

Maura didn't answer but fought back hot tears. She forced herself to concentrate on how Millie stroked her hair after each pull with Mother's comb. Finally, she decided that Millie combed her hair as well as Mother, even if she did not hum.

"I miss Mother and Father," said Maura. "Do you think that means I'm weak?"

"Of course not," replied Millie. "I miss them too."

The girls were quiet after that, both recalling some fond memory of home.

When they had finished combing, Millie cut a few pieces from the hanging moose meat and boiled them. Millie and Maura ate some, then gave the rest of the tasty soup to the dogs.

The man returned before dark with a fat beaver,

which he quickly skinned outside, giving the dogs the thick, flat tail. Dogs love to chew on beaver tails. For supper the man rolled chunks of the dark beaver meat in flour and fried them. He also mixed a batch of batter, which he fried in the splattering grease. The cabin smelled delicious. Maura liked the fried bread so much that she snuck a piece into her dress pocket along with a chunk of beaver meat.

The man took down a bottle from a shelf above his bed. He took a long drink from it and then offered it to Millie, who took and sip and almost spat it out. The clear liquid burned her throat and tongue.

"That's terrible," she said, her face twisted in disgust. She wiped her mouth with her sleeve.

The man laughed at her expression, grabbed the bottle from her, and took another drink.

After supper the man brought the beaver pelt inside to scrape clean on a tanning board. Millie grew agitated watching him. His method of scraping the pelt was not right, not what she had learned from watching her father. Maura didn't seem to notice.

When the man was finished with his chore, he played his musical instrument again, stopping often to drink from the bottle, which was now half empty. His eyes were glassy and he swayed on the edge of the bed as if he wasn't able to sit up straight.

The girls visited the outhouse before bedtime. The night was cold, the sky star-filled, the snowy landscape brightened by a full moon hanging high above the hills. Both girls fell asleep quickly after slipping into their bedding.

Millie was startled in the middle of the night. She opened her eyes, and although it was dark in the cabin, she could see the man on his knees beside her, one hand outstretched. His hairy arms and face reminded her again of the frightful stories of Bush Indians.

He put a finger to his lips.

Millie cried out and tried to wriggle away, but the man held her by the shoulders, speaking to her softly. The shout startled Maura, though, who awoke confused and frightened.

"He tried to touch me!" Millie cried in their language, her voice shaky, terrified.

The giant man stood up, grabbed Millie by an arm, and yanked her upright. He flung her to his narrow bed, bending over her, trying to grab her arms as she kicked and scratched and pleaded for her sister to help her. The dogs were barking outside.

Maura could not think, only act. She seized a heavy piece of split firewood from beside the stove and struck the man on the temple with all her might. Anger and terror drove her blow, and the sound was like a spruce limb snapping under the weight of snow. The man collapsed, unconscious, atop Millie, who struggled to get out from beneath his bulk.

Millie grabbed her rifle, loaded a round into the chamber, aimed at the motionless man, and told her sister to dress quickly and to roll up their bedding. The man was making groaning sounds. When Maura was clothed and had donned her parka and mukluks, Millie handed the rifle to her sister while she quickly dressed, flung the bundled tarp over her shoulder, and took back the rifle.

The huge man was trying to lift himself just as they opened the door to leave. Abandoning caution, the girls scrambled down the bank and onto the frozen river.

"Go! Go!" Millie cried. "I'll wait until you get halfway across—otherwise, the ice could break."

The light dogs ran ahead, careless of everything but the excitement of a late-night romp. Over another freezing night and day, the ice had thickened slightly; it crackled but held under their racing mukluks. Just as Maura reached the safety of the far bank and Millie reached the middle of the river, they heard the man yelling at them. Drunk as he was, he was running onto the ice, calling, "Come back here!"

Tundra, his hackles suddenly bristling, turned and ran at him barking, his ears pulled back. He looked like a wolf.

"Tundra, no!" Maura cried. "Come back!"

"Keep running!" Millie shouted to her sister. She prayed to that deceiver Raven that the ice would not support the man's weight.

As Millie also reached the far bank, they heard a cracking sound, like the fracturing of the trunk of a great tree in a storm. They turned to see Tundra, his jaws latched to the man's thigh, and the giant scrambling in the shattering ice. The man and dog splashed into the river.

The girls watched the two struggling to get out from the icy water. But the ice was too thin. Each time the man tried to pull himself out, it gave way and he'd go under again. Nor could Tundra escape. He vanished as Maura screamed his name.

While the giant was trying to save himself, Millie and Maura kept running, clambering up the bank onto the trail they had been traveling on before. Blue trotted beside them, stopping frequently to look behind him. Then he'd turn and race to catch up with the girls. For a long way they could hear the man shouting. They kept running, afraid that the hairy-faced giant was behind them.

Parents had been right to warn their children of monsters in the forest.

Nadaeggi Uk'edi
(Twelve)

For the rest of the spring and summer, Raven taught the woman how to catch fish in fish traps. He showed her how to build a suitable dwelling, how to make fire, and where to find bird eggs and edible berries.

THE SISTERS PITCHED no camp that night, convinced that every rustling branch was the shaggy man creeping up on them. They didn't know if he had escaped the river.

Blue stayed close to Maura's side.

Instead, they built a fire beneath the shelter of a wide-limbed spruce tree and sat wrapped in blankets on a pile of green boughs with their backs to the trunk, the loaded rifle across Millie's lap. The untended fire died as they napped, and Blue occasionally whined in his sleep. While they slept, the temperature rose somewhat and low clouds slipped into the windless valley, concealed the gleaming moon, and released a foot of snow without a sound.

The girls awoke in the morning, astounded that so much snow had fallen during the night. Millie rebuilt the fire, breaking dry, needleless branches above her and feeding the small but hungry flames a handful at a time. While they hunched close to the growing fire, Millie and Maura wept for the loss of Tundra. They had saved him from the raging river, but the river took him nonetheless. Between those two moments, he had helped them, protected them, maybe even saved their lives.

After sharing the fried bread and the piece of beaver that Maura had stuffed in her pocket, the girls rolled up their bedding, helped each other into their burdensome packs, and started off downriver again—the going made more difficult by the foot of powdery new snow on top of the crusted snow that had fallen several days earlier. They were both grateful for their mukluks and the skill with which their mother and aunt had made them to keep their feet warm and dry.

So early, the entire world was still sleeping beneath the white blanket. Only a curious raven moved on the silent land, following the three travelers, watching them from one treetop and then another, until he finally flew away to search for something to eat, cawing his lonely name.

Gaw gok! Gaw gok!

Late in the afternoon they mounted a ridge overlooking the village the Indian guide had said was plagued by death. They had known, from comments their father and uncles had often made, approximately how far downriver it was from their own village. Bend after meandering bend in the river, they had been expecting to find it.

But it was not what they had hoped.

Nothing moved except wagging tree limbs unburdening themselves of new snow in the rising wind. No smoke rose from the houses. No dogs or children ran out to greet them. No tracks disturbed the bright, thick blanket of new-fallen snow. The whole village, which was slightly larger than their own, was as quiet and as white as a ghost.

"There's no one here," Millie said.

Maura did not respond. The two girls stood for several

minutes taking in the scene. Most of the cabin doors stood open, frozen amid drifts.

Millie and Maura had often wondered about the village during their journey, whispering about it at night around the campfire, as if they were afraid to speak of it aloud. They worried that if the man from this village had carried the red spots up to their village, then it stood to reason that the sickness could have killed everyone here too. They didn't know what they would find or if anyone would still be alive. They knew only that they couldn't stay home. They had to find other people. They couldn't survive for long on their own.

Finally, Millie began tramping down the ridge toward the houses. Maura followed in her tracks, having learned that it was easier to walk in her sister's broken trail. They stopped beside a salmon-drying rack just like the ones in their own village.

"No one here," Millie repeated softly, to herself or to the air, the wind blowing her hair in her face.

Maura took her sister's hand. Blue sat between them.

"Where are all the people?" Maura asked, squeezing Millie's fingers.

As much as they had feared it, neither sister had

actually expected to find the village as dead as their own. The sickness had been here first, but this was a larger village. They had hoped to find survivors like themselves.

"They're all dead," Millie said. "The spotted plague has killed all of them, just as it did in our village."

Maura began to shake a little. The bitter wind seemed to creep into her clothes, into her bones.

Not again, she thought. *Not everyone.*

Millie and Maura imagined the last days of life in this village. Had starving dogs consumed the dead? Had the bears come? Were there any survivors who left to go downriver in search of the white settlement? Was the deep, mounded snow concealing half-burned corpses?

"What do we do now?" Maura asked. "Is everyone dead everywhere?"

Millie thought about that for several moments before she answered.

"I don't know. I just know that we have to keep going. We have to look for others. We have to find the trading settlement where the rivers join. From the way Father described it, most of the people who live there are white." The sisters remembered how the two white strangers were not sick when they left their village. "Surely there are people alive there—people kind enough to take us in, maybe even some of our own people who also survived the sickness."

"How far away is that?" asked Maura, looking up at Millie the way she used to look at her mother when she needed to know something.

"A long ways, I guess. We may be only halfway there, maybe not even that close. But we have to keep going," Millie replied, suddenly tired. She wanted to be the one to ask questions, to hear answers.

"Everything is so still," Maura whispered.

Strangely, the buried cabins looked peaceful beneath the clean, trackless snow. The three trudged through the empty village, avoiding looking into each house, fearful of what they might find. They had seen enough of death.

"Do you think there are ghosts here?" asked Maura, staying close to her sister, remembering the timid spirit of the drowned man they had seen running across treetops.

"I don't know."

"Do you think Mother and Father are ghosts?" she asked.

"I don't know. . . . Maybe," replied Millie.

"Do you think they would remember us?" Maura asked, wiping away a streaming tear with a parka sleeve.

"I think so."

"Do you think they miss us?"

"Yes," Millie answered, mostly because *she* missed them so much.

The girls wondered if the spirits wandering the village were fearful for the safety of the two living girls. Millie wondered if the wind, rising to a howl, was made by the shouts of the dead warning them to run away before the red spots awakened. Maura wondered about her own abandoned village. Did it look like this one now, the blasting wind off the lake breathing darkly in long, hard breaths through open doors? Were the dead there buried beneath a peaceful blanket of snow?

Although the girls were too frightened to enter any of the deserted homes, which now belonged to the wind and the drifting snow, they peeked inside every cache, climbing the rickety ladders. In the back of one, they found a bundle of dried salmon, which looked as though ravens had pecked at it. But the meat was still good. They split the fish equally, tucking them securely inside their packs. Millie also took two pairs of snowshoes from the wall outside a cabin, figuring the spirits would not begrudge her. After all, it was a long way to the trading settlement far below, where the two rivers meet.

Winter would accompany them on their journey.

Less than a mile downriver, the trail came to a wide, snow-covered creek, which emptied into the river. The white surface lay undisturbed. It was the broadest creek they had encountered on their journey. Others had been little more than rills, near empty in winter, easy to traverse. This one was at least thirty feet across, maybe more. But it didn't look dangerous.

Besides, they couldn't go around it.

Halfway across, Millie and Maura sank up to their waists in overflow, one of the most dangerous natural phenomena in the far North. Sometimes water runs over the surface of ice on a creek or river or lake, hidden beneath deep and undisturbed snow, a sinister and secret trap.

The sisters struggled to get out of the slush. The snowshoes were too heavy to lift, and the girls had to lean down until the water nearly reached their shoulders to remove them, even as they stood in the ice-cold overflow. Blue struggled, too. Luckily, their packs did not get wet. When the girls reached the opposite side, they knew the danger they were in. Maura cried from the pain in her hands and feet. She was freezing, holding her arms across her chest and shivering. Millie made her crouch on the wind-protected side of a tree while she, with numbing fingers, fumbled to build a fire.

They both knew plenty of stories about the perils of overflow.

Their grandfather had lost all of his toes after his dogsled got stuck in overflow on a creek. He had been checking a trap line when the dogs and the sled sank into the slush. It was thirty degrees below zero—more than sixty degrees colder than freezing. For half an hour he struggled to pull the dogs and sled out of the overflow, scraping the freezing slush from the runners.

Then he made a mistake.

Instead of immediately building a fire to dry his clothes and the dogs' feet, he pushed for home, ten miles away. By the time he arrived, his leggings and boots were frozen solid. When his family pulled off his boots, his toes were black and dead. They had to be amputated. Two of the dogs had to be put down; their paws had frozen, too.

Overflow was a serious matter.

As soon as Millie had a fire going, she broke branches from beneath a spruce tree and fashioned a lean-to by using the tarp and a pole propped against the tree. For the rest of the night they huddled naked beneath blankets, feeding the fire, drying their clothes and mukluks.

Blue lay nearby, licking his wet fur and using his front teeth to pull chunks of ice from between his splayed paws.

Taaʻí Uḵʻedi

(Thirteen)

Raven taught the woman how to use a bow and arrow to hunt game. He showed her how to snare rabbits. He even instructed her how to trap beaver and muskrat and how to fashion warm clothing from their pelts.

A BLIZZARD ASSAILED the valley by morning, the heavy snowflakes swirling on a hard wind that seemed to blow from every direction. The whiteout was so complete that Millie and Maura could barely see ahead, and the twisting and drifting snow quickly covered the light footprints of their snowshoes. The stinging flakes clung to eyebrows and froze eyelashes so that the girls had to rub ice from their eyes to see.

Several times they thought they had lost Blue, but the dog returned when Millie shouted or Maura whistled.

The sisters walked all day, without taking much notice of their surroundings, mindlessly putting one snowshoe in front of the other, deep in distracting thoughts and day-dreams. They thought about the happy past before the sickness came to their village. They thought about the dead village behind them. And they wondered if they would ever reach the white settlement. They wondered what they would do if they found it abandoned, too. Where would they go from there? How would they live?

All day the snow kept falling, getting deeper, making the going difficult for Blue, who sank up to his belly. Their only bearing was the river. Wherever possible, they walked along its treeless bank or beneath trees at the forest's edge. They stopped only once to rest beneath a close stand of spruce trees, which offered some protection against the storm. Millie managed to make a fire, first kicking away the snow to expose the frozen ground, crouching over her little glass jar of matches, the striker, and strips of white, paper-thin bark, which she had peeled off a birch tree earlier in the day. As the flames grew, she carefully added dry pinecones and twigs, warily shielding the fire from the wind, which constantly threatened to extinguish the flames. She melted some snow in the pot, adding pieces of dried salmon to the boiling water, making a tasty fish broth. After the girls drank their fill, Blue licked what remained in the pot.

After the brief respite, the threesome journeyed on down the river and into the gathering dusk, looking for a place to camp for the night. As always, Maura straggled behind. She was, after all, younger than Millie, and her legs were shorter. Besides, the long and heavy snowshoes were meant for a much taller adult.

Without signaling Millie, Maura stopped to relieve her bladder. She would be quick about it. She squatted on the trail a hundred feet below a fork where the river trail intersected a well-used game trail. Unaware that Maura had stopped, Millie plodded on, vanishing in the storm. Blue stayed with Maura, his back covered with snow. He shook himself and sniffed the base of a swaying birch tree and then left his own scent on the trunk.

Millie had taken the trail that most appeared to follow the river, which she could not see through the trees and snow but knew was there, just out of sight to her left. The other trail curved abruptly at an angle away from the river, toward a flat valley between hills. She passed the fork without much consideration and without looking back, assuming that, as always, Maura and the dog were right behind her. The wind roared in the trees above, something between a whistle and a moan, and the snow continued unabated.

After Millie had walked for another half hour absorbed in her own thoughts, she stopped and looked back for the first time since passing the fork. Her sister was not there. She stood on the trail for a while, peering into the dark, expecting Maura and Blue to emerge from around the bend. As she waited, she pulled a strip of dried salmon from her parka and chewed on it slowly, enjoying the flavor of the oily red meat. She saved the silvery skin for Blue.

At last, Millie walked back around the bend and looked down a straight stretch. Snow was falling so heavily that she could see only halfway down the trail. Neither Maura nor the dog was visible. She walked down the stretch until she could see the trail's bend with the river. Still nothing.

Millie cupped her hands around her mouth and shouted her sister's name several times, holding her breath after each shout and listening for a reply. It was so quiet that she could hear snowflakes landing on her parka hood. She wiped her eyelashes and yelled again.

"M-a-u-r-a! M-a-u-r-a!"

She tried to whistle like her father and sister, but she had never learned that art. She made a kind of whistling noise, no louder than the rush of breath escaping around her tongue.

Suddenly, Millie felt sure that something had stolen her sister, perhaps wolves or a sleepless bear or angry spirits from the dead village. Perhaps the hairy-faced giant had survived the river after all and had taken his revenge on Maura and on Blue.

Millie shuddered, more from fear than from the cold.

But she had heard no sounds of struggle. Surely she would have heard Blue barking or Maura screaming.

Millie ran down the trail as fast as she could on the snowshoes, the bundled tarp bouncing against her back, the slung rifle sliding off her shoulder. She fell twice. When she had returned to the fork, there was no sign of her sister or the dog, no disturbance on the snow whatsoever to indicate their passing. Millie remembered the last time she had seen Maura was half a mile or more upriver from the trail junction, where they'd had to step around a large tree that had fallen across the trail.

Although it was already dark, she set off briskly upriver, in the wrong direction.

✦　✦　✦

When Maura came to the fork, the wind was blowing so hard that she had to lean into it and turn her face away from its might, squinting hard; otherwise, the snow stung her eyes so badly that she could barely keep them open. Blue, smelling some scent, maybe of a moose or a wolf or another porcupine, took off down the trail to the right, the wrong direction, and Maura followed without question. She hadn't noticed the other trail at all, assuming that while the fury of the storm might impede her sight, it surely did not hinder the dog's keen sense of smell. Maura was certain that Blue was following Millie. And although she was exhausted from the long day's march, she quickened her pace to catch up, knowing that her sister was only a minute or two ahead, just around the next bend.

Within half an hour it was dark. The clouds were thick and angry, racing above the valley, hurling snow at the world.

Maura began calling Millie's name, her tumbling words deadened on the fierce wind. She was crying, afraid of being alone in the wilderness—now she understood how Millie must have felt when she wandered off to pick berries. The tears only made her cheeks cold and her eyelashes freeze faster. She couldn't imagine that her sister could be so far ahead of her. Maura had stopped only for a couple of minutes. And she had been hurrying ever since. She should have caught up well before now. What had happened?

After walking a little farther, she decided to stop and wait for Millie, who would surely notice that she was missing and turn back to find her. Millie was okay. She *had* to be. And Millie was strong and capable and organized. She *would* find Maura. This was a good plan. Maura's father had taught her that when a person is lost in the woods, it is sometimes best to stop walking, which only makes matters worse. Besides, it was so dark and the storm so unrelenting that she might easily step off the trail and find herself in the middle of nowhere.

Blue, who had been leading the way, sat down beside her.

Maura kicked away snow from beneath the base of a spruce tree alongside the trail. She managed to break off a few low-reaching green boughs from neighboring trees, and she piled them on the ground as an insulating pallet, preventing the frozen ground from sapping her warmth. After untying her bundle, she called Blue over to her, and they snuggled under the blankets, sharing a piece of dried salmon and their body heat. There would be no fire or windbreak. Millie had the matches and the tarp.

Maura wondered if she and Blue could survive the night huddled as they were under blankets. Already Maura's toes and fingers were tingling with the onset of numbness. Maura wondered where Millie was and how she could outlast the night without blankets. She wondered why Millie wouldn't have stopped on the trail at some point and waited for her. Had she accidentally stepped off the trail and gotten lost? Was she somehow behind them? If so, would she soon catch up?

Had something terrible happened to Millie?

Maura held the dog close.

"Millie will come looking for us," she whispered sadly.

Blue licked her face.

"Don't worry, boy. She'll find us."

Finding no sign of her sister or Blue at the deadfall where she had last seen Maura, Millie could only conclude that Maura had taken the wrong trail at the junction behind her. Millie calculated that Maura and Blue could be miles up that trail by now. She decided to return to the fork and spend the night. Perhaps Maura would realize her error and turn around.

By the time she arrived where the two trails split, Millie was very tired, not simply from the day's labor, but also from worry and a growing horror that her little sister might be freezing to death. It was too dangerous to travel any farther. In the darkness and storm she might accidentally step off the trail and get lost. Besides, if Maura turned back, she'd have to come to this point. Millie built a lean-to using the tarp and sat beneath it beside a crackling fire, watching the swirling snow and listening for her sister. She got up many times to collect more firewood, each time shouting Maura's name. Only the sound of trees creaking in the wind answered.

The long night passed slowly for Millie, who was afraid to fall asleep and let the fire die, afraid that her sister might inadvertently pass her in the darkness. She wondered if Maura would know enough to turn back or at least to stop and wait, or was she still out there wandering farther and farther as she struggled to find her older sister?

Sometime long after midnight, the blizzard slackened and finally passed. In the terrible silence Millie fought off images of Maura frozen beneath the snow. Why had she allowed her to get lost? What would she say to her mother's spirit when they met and the terrible question would come: *Why did you abandon your sister?*

In the morning, she shook snow from the tarp, folded it, and carefully tucked the blackened cooking pot and the jar of matches inside the bundle. When she was done, she tied it into a pack, slung it over her back, and jumped lightly to adjust the load. She strapped on the snowshoes, took up her rifle, and started down the game trail that led away from the river, in search of her sister.

Not long after leaving the fork, Millie encountered a pack of five wolves. At first they kept their distance, curiously observing the girl from behind trees. But then they grew more daring, encircling her, snarling and growling and snapping their teeth. Millie worked the lever of her father's rifle and fired a warning shot into the air, startling the wolves, which bolted back into the trees. Millie kept trudging down the trail, holding the rifle ready, alert to any movement around her.

After regaining their courage, the pack began to stalk her again, more wary this time.

Millie aimed at the closest wolf, a dark-colored dominant male—the pack leader, most likely. She pulled the trigger and just missed hitting the animal in the head. This time the wolves ran away in the direction Millie was heading, in the direction of her sister.

Maura awoke to the sound of a rifle shot echoing in the hills. She and Blue, huddled together in a mound of snow-covered blankets, had not moved all night. She sat upright and listened. The sky was cloudless, and she could clearly see the surrounding hills. A few minutes later, she heard another shot. Blue pricked his ears in that direction.

Millie, Maura thought as she jumped up and stood looking down the trail. Her feet were numb, but her hands were warm. She had entangled her fingers in Blue's thick fur as she slept.

Quickly, she rolled up the blankets, bound them tightly, and threw the bedroll over her shoulder. She laid both snowshoes flat, stepped onto one, secured the strapping across her mukluk, and then put on the other. The movement made her toes tingle, which was good, she thought. They had feeling, which meant they weren't frostbitten. She could wiggle them slightly in her mukluks. As soon as she was ready, having donned her thick mittens, Maura took up her walking stick and set off in search of her sister. Blue was at her side, struggling in the deep snow.

A little ways down the trail, a pack of wolves emerged from around a bend. At first they did not see the two, but suddenly they stopped, stared hard at the girl and the dog at her side, and then dashed after them, kicking up snow as they ran. A dark-colored wolf was in the lead, his tongue hanging out of his mouth as he bounded toward them.

Blue started barking and raced for the wolves.

"No, Blue! Wait!" Maura shouted.

She swallowed her panic and felt a hot wave of anger flow up her back and into her arms. Not even five feet tall, Maura took the hatchet from her rope belt and waited, the hatchet in one hand and her walking stick in the other. Blue launched into the lead wolf when it was close. The two canines clashed in a fury of dark fur and teeth. It was difficult to tell them apart. The other wolves watched with a kind of detachment, keeping their distance and yelping among themselves.

"Blue!" shouted Maura, trying to call the dog to her. "Blue!"

Wolves often kill and eat village dogs. It happened every winter. Though terrified for Blue and for her own safety, Maura stood her ground and screamed at the wolf.

"Stop it! Get! Get!"

The valley echoed with the sounds of the furious battle. Another of the wolves suddenly charged at Maura, who struck it across the nose with her staff. The wolf yelped and retreated, frantically rubbing its snout between its paws.

"Get out of here!" Maura screamed again and again, waving the long walking stick, desperately trying to frighten away the wolves, which paid little attention to her.

Just then Millie came around the bend. She was out of breath, having run for a long time after hearing the ruckus. From where she stood, she could see her sister shouting and swinging her staff to keep the wolves at bay. She could also see Blue tangling with the same lead wolf she had shot at and missed earlier. Although she was far away, Millie fired her rifle into the air. The wolves turned and saw her. She fired again, and they ran away as they had done before, into the wooded hills, bounding through the deep snow. Hurriedly, she loaded several bullets from her pocket into the rifle and ran toward her sister.

Blue was lying in a circle of trampled and bloodied snow, whimpering and bleeding from several wounds. Maura knelt beside him, holding his head and crying, speaking gently to the dog, stroking his wet and matted fur. By the time Millie reached her sister, Blue was dead. He had protected Maura the way Tundra had protected them both from the terrible man. Maura stood up and clutched her sister, her body trembling as she sobbed aloud.

"Oh, Millie, he gave his life to save me."

Although it arced closer to the horizon than to the vaulted sky, the sun was bright on the deep, new snow. A raven cawed as it flew from the hills toward the river. A white hare, which had come out of its hole to see what the commotion was, hopped behind a stand of willows. The two sisters stood hugging each other for a long time.

Neither spoke a word. There was little to say. Both wondered what they would have done without the other.

When they were ready, the sisters set off for the fork in the trail, where they would continue downriver to the trading settlement they had never seen. As they had been at the very beginning of their journey, Millie and Maura were again alone.

Denc'i Uk'edi

(Fourteen)

Because of Raven's kindness, the woman was able to feed her children. Many years later, when the three boys had become strong young men, they returned to their old village during a time of famine. The people were starving.

THE TEMPERATURE DROPPED quickly after the storm. By the afternoon of the second day, it was already twenty degrees below zero, maybe colder, dangerous conditions for moving about.

As usual, Millie was leading the way, breaking trail in the deep snow. She was sweating from the labor, the perspiration making her clothes wet against her skin. And although the exertion warmed her at the moment, the wetness quickly robbed her clothing of the ability to insulate her whenever she stopped moving.

If she had known better, Millie would have opened the front of her parka to cool down or removed it altogether, the way her father did when he cut or split firewood in the front yard. But she was too inexperienced in the wilderness to realize the danger of wetness in below-zero weather. Her father knew it. Her uncles knew it. Anyone who labored in the north in winter understood the danger. The sisters understood cold. For most of the year, the cold was their world. But they hadn't yet faced this particular danger themselves. Whenever they'd broken into a sweat outdoors—playing or helping Mother or Father with a chore—they'd been in their village, just steps away from a warm home where their clothes could dry out.

As Millie walked ahead of her sister on the frozen river, shivering whenever she stopped to rest even for a few minutes, she began to see caribou tracks, hundreds of them. A great herd had moved through the area, crossing the river. Because it had snowed only two days before, she knew that the tracks were fresh. She also knew that the herds, some of thousands of migrating animals, take days to pass through a region. Stragglers often wander around for weeks after the main herd has moved on, easy pickings for wolves. Millie slid the rifle from her shoulder as she walked, eagerly scanning the forest ahead.

"Maybe we'll get a caribou," she said.

Millie tried to sound confident to help keep Maura's, and her own, spirits as high as possible. But she was beginning to lose hope. They had found no survivors in the village behind them, and she had no idea how far it was to the white settlement. What if it was too far? She worried that winter would only become colder and colder every day. What if it reached sixty below, which wasn't uncommon for this time of year? Could they survive the cold? She was tired of walking, and Maura— little as she was—must be even more exhausted.

"Let's keep a sharp eye," she said.

Maura liked the idea. Caribou meat tastes different from moose meat. People usually prefer one over the other, and caribou was Maura's favorite. When the girls walked around the bend, sure enough, they saw a small band of caribou milling around on the frozen river.

"Stop," Millie whispered, holding up a hand.

Eight caribou, mostly cows, scuffed the snow away from the river's ice coat with their small antlers, looking for grass or moss. Bulls lose their antlers each year after the mating season in late fall, but cows keep theirs to scrape snow from the ground in search of food and to protect their young. Two young bulls were walking amid the cows.

The girls eased a little closer—Maura stooped immediately behind her bigger sister, placing her feet exactly in Millie's tracks—so that Millie had a better chance of sneaking up on them. They moved slowly, keeping out of sight by staying in line with a brushy deadfall by the river's frozen edge. Several times they stopped, thinking a caribou was looking their way. When they were crouched behind the deadfall, Millie pulled off her right glove with her teeth and slowly worked the rifle's lever, which was stiff from the cold. Though she was shivering, she aimed carefully and pulled the trigger.

Nothing happened. She pulled back the hammer, aimed again, and squeezed the trigger.

It was so cold that the firing pin would not slide freely. In such cold weather, experienced hunters know to wipe excess grease and oil from all moving parts. At twenty below, even oily lubricants freeze. But Millie, as a girl, was not an experienced hunter. In fact, as a girl, she had never been allowed to hunt with her father.

The caribou were slowly making their way across the

river. In another moment, they would reach the tree line on the other side and she would miss her chance. Just then, one of the bulls stopped and stood sideways to the girls, an easy target.

"Hurry, Millie," Maura whispered excitedly.

"I'm trying," replied Millie, working the lever again, ejecting the unfired bullet into the snow and manually feeding another one into the chamber. Millie didn't realize it, but the motion of the hammer twice striking the firing pin loosened the frozen oil, allowing it to move freely.

She aimed at the broad side of the caribou, held her breath, and pulled the trigger. This time the rifle went off in a cloud of smoke and jerked hard against her shoulder. The small bull caribou jumped away, ran a few steps, and stumbled. It fell over, kicked for several seconds, and then lay still. The rest of the band had bolted into the forest.

"You did it, Millie! You did it!" Maura shouted and clapped her hands. "What a great shot! You're a real hunter."

She was more excited than Millie, who stood smiling, the slight wind blowing her hair across her face.

The girls ran out on the frozen river and stood over

the dead caribou. It was Millie's first big-game kill—the first time she had successfully hunted with a gun. In happier times, if she had been a boy, the village would have celebrated such an occasion. But on the wintered river, the sisters celebrated in their own way, skinning back the hide to expose the meat on a hindquarter. The rump showed a good deal of fat, the sign of a healthy animal that has eaten well to prepare for winter.

Millie butchered the caribou while Maura gathered firewood and built a fire on the riverbank, carefully using the matches and tinder the way Millie had taught her, the way their father had taught Millie. Because they had no way of carrying all the meat, Millie cut several thick pieces from the rump and stuffed them inside the folded tarp. While she worked with the knife, her shivering increased. The skin parka was trapping the moisture, and her wet clothes were beginning to freeze. If she had known better, Millie would have removed her parka and dried her damp clothing over the fire, but she thought that maybe she was coming down with a fever and so she stayed bundled up.

When the butchering was finished, the girls cooked some of the meat on short willow sticks.

"Blue and Tundra would have liked this," Maura said

before biting off a piece of meat that was cooked on the outside. The inside was still red.

A raven flew down and landed on the ground nearby. It hopped closer to the fire and cocked its black head, looking at the girls.

"Here, Raven," Millie said, tossing a piece of meat to the bird, which hopped sideways but did not fly off.

Perhaps their good fortune was the bird's doing. After all, Millie recalled being told stories, albeit few, in which Raven helped people in need. In one, a young woman and her children are lost in the wilderness, close to death. Raven takes pity on the woman and teaches her how to hunt and fish and how to build a shelter for her family. It was one of the few Raven stories Millie could remember with a happy ending.

Millie wondered if Raven had helped her and Maura escape the wolves and the giant, hairy man. Did Raven entice the small bull caribou to turn sideways just when he could have escaped into the forest?

The raven snatched the bit of meat, stared at the girls, blinked, and then flew away and landed on a nearby tree. Millie cut several small pieces, which she tossed to the bird each time it flew down from the tree.

As the already low sun began sinking below the distant horizon, the girls could tell from the clear sky that the night was going to be very cold. They thought about camping where they were, which seemed to be as good a place as any, but Maura pointed out that the caribou carcass might attract wolves. Millie agreed. They decided to walk downriver some distance and then make camp.

Millie was getting deep-down cold, bone cold, from her wet clothes. But they soon found a perfect spot. The wind had long ago uprooted a large, dead spruce tree. Because spruce tree roots do not go deep, they frequently rip out of the ground fully attached to their trunk when a tree falls, forming a semicircular wall of shallow roots entangled in thick soil, sometimes as tall as seven or eight feet. The branches of the tree were dry and brittle, a convenient supply both of firewood and, when trimmed a little with the hatchet, of shelter poles.

Millie and Maura built a shelter against the earthen wall using a row of equally spaced poles over which they spread the tarp, covering it with a foot or more of snow. In very cold weather, snow acts as insulation against wind and cold. While the wind may howl and drive temperatures to fifty degrees below zero outside an Arctic igloo, the inside can stay eighty degrees warmer from the simple use of oil lamps for light and heat. Then the sisters gathered green boughs from neighboring spruce trees and piled them on the floor of their home to raise their bodies off the frozen ground. When they were satisfied with their shelter, the best they had ever built, the girls stacked a supply of firewood by gathering up all the small branches they had trimmed from the poles.

From a distance, the snow-covered shelter was indiscernible from the wintered surroundings, a snowdrift against a fallen tree.

The girls sat beside a little fire within their makeshift shelter, melting snow for drinking water and caribou soup. They had to keep the fire small to avoid burning a hole through the tarp. There was enough draft to allow smoke to escape. It was so cold outside that the fire could only warm the interior to around freezing, which, though uncomfortable, was far better than twenty or thirty below. The girls had to wear their parkas and mukluks and gloves. They went outside only to gather more wood or to relieve themselves.

The frantic northern lights and innumerable stars filled the sky.

The sisters could hear the sharp sound of trees popping. At very low temperatures, the moisture inside trees freezes and bursts the wood's sinews; the exploding sound is like that of a rifle fired in the distance. It was far too cold to travel.

With little else to do inside their shelter, and knowing that cold spells sometimes lasted for many days, weeks even, the girls talked and retold stories they had heard all their lives, ancient stories about when animals spoke and acted like people *before* there were people. Every tale offered something to be learned. Millie recalled the stories easily, and Maura enjoyed seeing bits and pieces of wisdom in them, things her mother had pointed to from time to time. Maura smiled thinly, remembering how sometimes Mother would end a tale saying, "When you are as clever as Fox, you can make your own way. Until then, you must listen to me."

Maura didn't just want to listen to her sister now, though. She also wanted to talk with her.

"Is Raven a real god, or are these just stories?" she asked.

Millie was slow to answer. She was feeling cold and clammy, in spite of the fire.

"Stories can be real," she replied. "They teach us things, like how to behave and how things came to be the way they are. Someday people may tell tales about how we survived the plague and winter. It will be a story about strength and courage."

They took turns telling other tales, occasionally correcting each other on minor points. Because stories are revered, it is important to tell them right.

"Do you think we will make it?" Maura asked after telling a story about how Raven once tricked Porcupine.

Millie thought about how far they had traveled, how they were already well beyond the downriver village, which, she thought, was possibly halfway to the trading settlement.

"Maybe," she answered, and then sipped some warm water from the pot.

"What if we don't make it?"

"Then we don't."

Millie's frankness was not comforting, and Maura became quiet for a long time. Finally, she broke the silence.

"What if we are alone for the rest of our lives, just the two of us in the whole world? What will become of us? Who will we marry?"

Millie responded to the question, although Maura already knew the answer.

"Then we shall never marry, and we shall never have children."

Maura started to cry. Certainly she was too young to worry about things like marriage, but she wanted to be like the other women in their village. She wanted a chin tattoo when she became of marrying age. She remembered touching her mother's tattoo on her deathbed. The notion that she might never marry—might never be like her mother—was too much. She lay down and pulled the blankets over her head and tried not to think about it.

Millie stared into the flames, adding handfuls of twigs while her sister slept. She had to stay awake. Someone had to tend to the fire. For both of them to sleep at the same time would be very dangerous.

But an hour later, the wetness on her back was a soggy burden, pulling out her body's heat, pushing her toward exhaustion. Cold and short of breath, she lay down, pulled the blankets close, and curled into a ball to conserve heat. Her body trembled, and she couldn't stop her teeth from chattering. She should wake Maura, but she didn't have the energy to speak or reach over to her. She didn't even have the energy to open her eyes.

As she fell asleep, an owl hooted outside. Millie wondered if it was speaking to her.

Maura awoke early in the morning to the feeling of something shaking against her. Millie was shivering uncontrollably. Maura sat up and tried to wake her sister. But no matter how much she called out or shook her, Millie did not respond. Her lips were blue-white, her quivering body as rigid as a corpse.

The fire was dead. No one had fed it.

Maura spread her own blankets over her sister and quickly built a small pile of twigs on the gray ashes of the campfire. She found the jar of matches and lit the pile, adding larger pieces as the flames grew steadily. More than half an hour passed before the fire warmed the interior so that Maura no longer saw her breath.

But despite the warmth, Millie was still shaking. Maura rubbed her sister vigorously, trying to warm her. Her mother had taught her how the friction of rubbing warms the muscles. She felt the wet clothing beneath the parka. With great effort, Maura undressed her sister and hung the wet clothes on a short root so they could dry. After rubbing Millie's arms, shoulders, and chest, she turned her over to rub her back and the backs of her legs, keeping a vigilant eye on the fire. The shaking slowed a little each time she made a pass up and down her sister's body. After an hour or two, Millie was no longer trembling.

After covering her sister with her own blanket, Maura went outside to break off more branches from the felled spruce tree. She gathered several armfuls, piling them within easy reach of the flap door. When she had collected enough to last the day, Maura crawled back inside the shelter and fed the fire, which had almost died completely again.

For the rest of the morning and afternoon, Maura tended the fire and lay beside Millie, nestling close, sharing her body heat and occasionally rubbing her sister's arms and legs to warm them. Sometimes Millie would open her eyes and stare quietly at Maura before drifting off again. At last, late in the day, she seemed for the first time to be completely awake. She turned her head away from Maura and looked all around the shelter, before turning back and croaking, "Where am I? What happened?"

Maura had spent the whole day desperately trying not to let herself think that her sister could be dying. She didn't want to imagine surviving without Millie. At that moment, Maura knew, finally, that Millie would live. She wanted to jump up and dance. She wanted to run outside and fling snow into the air. She wanted to kiss Millie softly on the forehead, the way Mother would have if she had been there.

Instead, she whispered, "You're all right now," then reheated the pot of caribou soup. Maura helped Millie to sit upright and drink the hot broth, which warmed her inside.

By evening, Millie's clothes were dry, and both girls were again telling stories. In the middle of a tale about Wolf and Fox, Millie stopped talking, her face turned serious.

"I almost ruined everything. If I had died, you would have been left alone," she said, the rims of her eyes beginning to turn red. "Thank you."

Maura took her hand and squeezed it gently. "We're sisters," she said, smiling.

Millie nodded in agreement, wiping away a tear. "Yes, sisters."

Maura started to say something, but Millie held up a hand, hushing her.

"A long time ago, I scolded you for fearing the waters

of the creek. I scolded you for being small and frightened. I told you that even though the badger is small, he frightens bears. You frighten me, sister. You must frighten bears. How strong you are. How wise and kind you are. I was wrong to think you weak and afraid."

The temperature stayed low for almost a week. Each tedious day seemed to last forever. The girls took turns sleeping and tending the fire, gathering firewood, and melting snow for drinking water and for making caribou soup. They talked when they were both awake. Eventually, as always before, the cold spell passed. Clouds arrived, the temperature rose, and the girls set off once again down the trail, glad to be moving, glad to be out of their shelter. As they trudged alongside the silent river, Maura led the way.

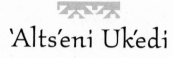

'Alts'eni Uk'edi

(Fifteen)

Because the mother had taught her sons all that
Raven had taught her, they were great hunters.
The three young men saved the village. Because
of their courage and their compassion to help
the old and weak, all three became great chiefs.
  Xay kuduldiye. *Let the winter be short.*
  Saan kuduset. *Let the summer be long.*

THE GIRLS WERE CERTAIN they were close to the trading settlement. They eagerly expected to see it every time they came around a bend. The white miles on the frozen river fell away quickly. But for days all they encountered as they trudged along was snow and ice and loneliness.

That suddenly changed one afternoon when the girls

saw a cabin at the far end of a long straight stretch. Maura was certain they had found the settlement.

"We're here!" she shouted. "We made it! We made it!"

Both girls quickened their pace, almost to a run. When they were close, they could see another cabin just around the bend.

Millie began to slow down.

"Come on!" Maura shouted gleefully. "We made it! We're saved!"

But Millie grabbed Maura's arm and yanked her to a standstill.

"Look," said Millie, standing on the snow-covered river looking up the steep bank at the first cabin. "There's no smoke coming from the roof."

Millie was right. There was no smoke rising from either cabin, no tracks in the deep snow around them. They climbed up the bank and looked inside the near one. It was empty. Pots and pans and blankets and all other belongings had been removed. Only a small, rusted woodstove remained.

They inspected the other cabin. It was also empty. They decided to spend the night in one of the cabins. Millie started a fire, and when the stove was hot, she set their cooking pot on top, filling it with snow to melt for drinking water. Then she placed several thin slices of caribou directly on the stove. The meat smelled delicious as it sizzled.

And though it was the most comfortable night they had experienced in a long time—since their first night at the bearded trapper's cabin—they slept poorly, tossed by their dreams. In Millie's nightmare, the warming fire was thawing the frozen plague, which waited hungrily in the walls. Maura dreamed of her mother, who had fallen into a dark cave and called over and over again for help. But Maura was unable to save Mother; her shouts became muffled and distant and then faded altogether. She woke with her heart pounding. It took a long time until she fell asleep again.

The next day they passed several more cabins, not collected together, as in a village, and each as empty as those before it. The girls grew disheartened.

"What if they're all empty?" Maura asked when they stopped to look inside a cabin with its door ajar and snow drifted a foot deep inside. She was beginning to believe that she and her sister really were the last two people alive.

"I don't know," replied Millie. "We've passed every landmark Father described. This should be the settlement. But where is everybody? Maybe they're all dead."

Millie was silent for a long beat. Then she said slowly, "But wait, Maura. Father often described the settlement as being many times bigger than our own village. All we've seen are a few cabins spaced far apart."

Maura's next words tumbled out. "He also said the settlement was where the two rivers come together, where this river joins a much larger one. We haven't seen any sign of the second river yet."

"That's true," Millie said, feeling slightly less anxious—but only slightly. They had traveled so far. She wanted to believe that they must be close. If so, the empty cabins could mean that the red spots had already killed everyone in this little community, then ravaged the village halfway upriver and finally their own—the most remote. By traveling downriver, the girls had been walking into the past, to where the spotted death had already come. Or maybe the lack of bodies and belongings in the cabins meant that the people hadn't died at all but moved to the white settlement, which must be nearby and would explain why the cabins were so empty. Millie breathed deeply.

Maura abruptly sat down on the trunk of a fallen tree. "Millie," she said, "what if everyone in the settlement is dead? What if it's also empty? What will we do then? Where will we go? Is there any point to going on? We could spend the rest of our lives looking for people. Why not just stay here, live our lives here, die here?"

"Stop it, Maura," replied Millie sharply. "We can't know where the trail goes until we travel it. This can't be the end of our walk. It's not the end of our lives. It's just not."

Millie sat down beside her sister, and despite her strong words, she began to shake. She didn't want to cry but couldn't help it. "Oh, please, Maura. Don't give up. We've come so far."

Maura stood, faced her older sister, pulled off her thick mittens, dropping them to the white ground, and cupped her warm hands around Millie's face.

"I'm sorry, Millie. I'm sorry. You're right. We have to keep going. I'll be like a badger again. I promise."

Millie rose and put her arms around Maura's waist, her cheek on her sister's head. The two sisters held each other until a groaning ice shift in the river broke the quiet.

"Let's go." Millie sighed and returned to the river, slowly breaking trail through the deep snow, opening her parka, being careful not to work up a sweat like before.

Abruptly, the valley began to narrow, turning into a steep, treeless canyon. The trail led up into the hills, and the sisters left the river to follow it. By nightfall, they made camp on a little point high above and overlooking the river. They built a great fire, for there was plenty of firewood, and sat around it for hours in silence—each preoccupied with worry.

While the stars gleamed and a waning moon momentarily slid behind a solitary silver cloud, the girls finished the last of the caribou meat. Then they huddled small and alone in the silence of the snow-covered land and the frozen river.

In the early afternoon of the next day, after trudging since sunrise, Millie and Maura came upon a clearing near the edge of a hill. Inside a fenced area, barely visible beneath the drifted snow, were dozens of miniature painted houses made of planks, most about five feet long and two or three feet tall. Some were smaller, but each was surrounded by a little white fence with a painted wooden cross erected behind the tiny house.

The girls had never before seen structures and crosses like these. Nevertheless, deep inside, they knew that this lonely field was a resting place for the dead—most likely for the inhabitants of the empty cabins they had passed along the river.

More and more, it seemed as if no one except Millie and Maura had escaped the plague. They alone would be Death's witnesses. Their perilous journey had been for nothing. The seemingly countless days and nights of hopeful suffering had been for nothing. The courageous deaths of Tundra and Blue had been for nothing.

They stood silently for a long time, leaning against the fence surrounding the little village of the dead. Millie struggled to find something to say, something that would lift their spirits.

Finally, she realized the truth. "Someone had to bury them."

She turned to Maura, to watch her expression. "There

must be someone alive. Surely there are people still alive somewhere."

Maura nodded. It did seem logical. They both looked again at the little houses. They wondered who would bury the two of them when they died; or would they simply lie exposed to the wild, like the carcass of the dead caribou?

At last they set off once again.

The trail leading away from the graveyard was wide. The girls had never seen such a wide trail cleared in the forest. Soon, it began to descend over the edge of the hill.

As they crested the hill, the girls stopped, astonished. Below them, the river they had been following for so long joined a much larger river, more than twice as wide. Portions of the great river were unfrozen. At the confluence were many dozens of buildings built close together, every one of them larger than any cabin the girls had ever seen, and every one of them puffing gray-white smoke into the air. Several taller buildings looked as though two or three cabins had been stacked on top of one another. There was also a large white building with a cross on its top, like those behind each tiny house at the cemetery. The girls could see people and dogs moving about. They could even hear sled dogs barking.

Millie and Maura stood on the hilltop for a long time, holding on to each other, a rising wind blowing their long black hair. Together, as they had been since the beginning, they ran down the hill as fast as their snowshoes could carry them, their packs bouncing hard against their backs, Millie's rifle sliding off her shoulder.